COMMANDING HER TRUST

Under His Command Trilogy

Part Two

By Lili Valente

D1522828

COMMANDING HER TRUST

Under His Command Trilogy: Part Two

Lili Valente

Table of Contents

About the Book

COMMANDING HER TRUST
Under His Command Book Two

*Warning: This book features a Dominant alpha man who will push your boundaries until you beg for more. Read at your own risk.
* *

Blake Roberts is falling hard for his old flame and won't stop until Erin is his. He doesn't simply want her body; he wants her submission, her abandon, and the wounded heart she's trying so hard to hide.

He wants all of her and he's pulling out all the stops—in the bedroom and out—until she surrenders.

For Erin, what started as a charade has become all too real. She's never experienced anything like the savage bliss she's discovered in Blake's arms. He tests her, dominates her, and if she doesn't gain her freedom, soon he'll own her—body and soul.

She has to escape even if running from Blake feels like running from the only home she's ever known.

Cliffhanger Alert: This steamy read ends in a cliffhanger. If you don't like being teased, steer clear. The entire UNDER HIS COMMAND series, Erin and Blake's complete love story, will publish in February and March of 2015.

Author's Note

Blake and Erin's story is a fictional representation of a Dominant and submissive, BDSM relationship, based on research conducted by the author. In a real Dominant and submissive relationship, all sexual activity should be safe, sane, and consensual.

Dedicated to my early readers.
Thank you for your time, enthusiasm, and all
around awesomeness.

ALSO BY LILI VALENTE

CONTROLLING HER PLEASURE

COMMANDING HER TRUST

CLAIMING HER HEART

Learn more at www.lilivalente.com

CHAPTER ONE

Blake

Blake watched the ancient pickup pull off onto the gravel at the road's edge and ran faster, determined to catch Erin before she got inside.

Before she took her life in her hands trying to get away from him.

It could be anyone in that truck. Some mountain man who hadn't seen a naked woman in years, a couple of drunk teenagers who would take turns raping the woman they'd picked up on the side of the road before dropping her off on the streets of San Bernardino. Or there could be a bona fide psychopath driving the vehicle: a man who would have his fun with Erin and then kill her, dumping her body in the surrounding wilderness where it might never be found.

Or maybe the driver is a nice grandmotherly type who will buy Erin some clothes before taking her to the police station to file a report against the man who kidnapped her.

Ahead of him, Erin ground to a stop, heels skidding across the asphalt.

"Help me, please, I…" She trailed off as an obese man in tattered overalls leveraged his considerable bulk out of the driver's side of the vehicle.

"You need help, darlin'?" He lurched forward, weaving his way toward the front of the truck, pursuing Erin as she backed away. "Happy to help a pretty thing like you."

Despite the chances of being convicted of a felony, a part of Blake wished it *had* been a sweet granny in the truck. Now he was probably going to come to blows with a man, who looked like an extra from *Deliverance*, to keep Erin safe. *And* he had a witness who might report what he'd seen to the authorities.

Not that it really mattered. If Erin decided she wanted to press charges, he wouldn't try to stop her. Despite what the voices in his head had been telling him lately, he wasn't a psychopath.

At least not yet. If this drunk did anything to Erin, however, he was going to lose what was left of his sanity in a memorable fashion.

"No one needs help." Blake's teeth ground together and something in his jaw popped as he watched one of the man's meaty hands reach toward Erin's chest. "Get back in your truck."

"I wasn't talking to you, asshole," the man said, still leering at Erin. "Come here, sugar and let me keep you warm."

"Get back in your truck," Blake repeated as his fingers closed around Erin's elbow. He pulled her behind him, shielding her nakedness with his body.

"Fuck off," Overalls said, beady eyes narrowing on Blake's face. "The lady asked for my help."

Blake cursed himself. Why had he told Erin to take off her shirt before getting out of the car? She was irresistible enough clothed.

Of course, he hadn't thought anyone else would see her. It was the middle of the night, for God's sake, and most people knew better than to try to navigate the treacherous mountain roads after dark, especially after hitting the bottle. But he could smell the whiskey on this character from three feet away.

Which gave him an idea...

"All right, don't get back in your truck," he said with a shrug. "I can smell the alcohol on your breath from here. And I doubt this will be your first DUI. Put your hands on the hood."

Blake heard Erin suck in a breath behind him as she caught on to what he was doing.

"I'm taking this one in for attempted prostitution," he added, jabbing a thumb over his shoulder. "It won't be any trouble to haul you into the station at the same time. I'll get her cuffed in the backseat and come back with some cuffs for you, Mr.…."

"Uh um…Beam. Walter Beam," the man said, backing toward the door to the battered pickup. "But I haven't been drinking, officer. I swear."

"Great. You can prove it when I get back with the Breathalyzer." Blake turned around, urging Erin in front of him, whispering as he went, "Get in the backseat."

"Prostitution?" she hissed, though she seemed relieved to have escaped "Mr. Beam's" attentions.

Mr. Beam. It didn't take much imagination to guess Beam was the brand of whiskey he'd been drinking, not the name on his license.

"Do I look like a prostitute?"

"I don't know. What does a prostitute look like?" Blake asked, not surprised to hear the pickup roar to life behind him and tires squeal as "Mr. Beam" took off down the mountain like a bat out of hell.

"I don't know, you're the one who lives in Vegas," she said, shivering as he opened the Expedition's door and urged her inside. "That was a sad cop act, by the way. I thought you had your own television show. I expected better than 'haul you into the station.' "

"It was a reality show. I just had to be myself, not act like anyone else." Blake reached into the front for Erin's bra and shirt and tossed them into her lap. "Put those on and don't run away from me again. You could have been seriously hurt."

"You've got to be kidding me." The car's overhead light illuminated Erin's face, revealing the flush that heated her cheeks. "*I* could have been hurt?"

"What do you think Walter would have

done to you?"

"I don't know," she said, with a frustrated huff. "Taken me back to town?"

Blake tipped his head. "Maybe, but not before he took advantage."

"Took advantage?" She laughed as she finished up with her bra, but her hands were shaking as she reached for her shirt. "He might have copped a feel. At most."

"He might have raped you," Blake said, anger making his voice even deeper.

"He might have tried," she said, returning his glare, making it clear she wasn't scared of his angry voice. "But I can take care of myself, Blake. In case you don't remember."

"Then why didn't you get in the truck with him?" he challenged. "If you were so sure he was a safe bet?"

"I guess I didn't want to see what you'd do to the poor guy if I did," she said, her eyes glittering in the dim light. "I mean, you're the person who's kidnapping a woman so he can make permanent alterations to her body. And you used to love *me*. Who knows what you might have done to some man you don't even know?"

The bravado in her tone made him sure she was simply reaching for the words that would hurt him the most, but they still cut deep. The way she'd known they would. She wasn't stupid, his Erin. Volatile, emotional, and often too impulsive for her own good, but never stupid.

"I did love you. Enough to believe everything you said to me the night before you ran away," Blake said, careful to keep the emotion out of his voice. "And I don't hate you now. I hope you know that. I don't want to hurt you."

"Tattooing someone against their will is bound to hurt," she said, her voice still hard, though he'd seen the flash of guilt on her face when he'd mentioned the night she'd fled Carson City. "Literally hurt, and probably do a pretty decent job of destroying any *trust* you've built with the woman you fucked against the hood of your car."

"Trust," he echoed, letting the word linger between them. "Is that was this is about? You regret letting me dominate you?"

Erin's eyes dropped to her fingers and she suddenly seemed very interested in the workings of the buttons on her shirt.

"Answer me," he insisted. "Do you regret what we did?"

She sucked in a deep breath and let it out on a sigh. "No," she mumbled, still not looking him in the eye.

"Then why did you run after we finished?" he asked, certain he was on to something. This wasn't about her trying to get away from him because she was afraid or didn't want her tat modified. It was about the power games they'd begun to play, the amount of trust she'd given him so readily.

The trust that had floored him, aroused him, and come closer to softening the walls he'd built around his heart than anything had. Anything or anyone, even Erin herself eight years ago. If he were a smart man, he'd turn the car around and take her back to Los Angeles right now.

No amount of ink modification was going to give him peace if he let Erin get under his skin again.

Too bad he was an idiot where this woman was concerned.

"Finished," she said, hurt clear in her tone. "That's a nice way to put it."

"I'm sorry. What do you want me to say?" Blake asked, ignoring the tightness that gripped his throat. "After we had sex?"

"Fucked would be fine. That's all it was, right?" She looked up, her face carefully blank. "A little fucking between friends?"

She was hurting, that was obvious—he wasn't fooled by her controlled expression. But how much of that pain had to do with what he'd done and how much was the result of her obviously troubled past, he couldn't say. But he could apologize, and try to make things as right between them as he could before they were holed up alone together for forty-eight hours.

"It was more than that. You know it, and so do I," he said. "I'm sorry if what we shared left you feeling confused, but you can't tell me you didn't enjoy it. Or that you didn't need it."

"You know nothing about what I need."

Blake sighed, recognizing her defiance for what it was, a mask for the fear many submissives felt when starting a relationship with someone new. He certainly hadn't meant to "start" anything or inspire those kinds of feelings in Erin, but now he had no choice but to deal with them.

"Listen, it's natural to be anxious about giving yourself over to another person, even if that person is someone you used to know very well," he said, keeping his tone soft and reassuring. He wanted her to know she was safe, that he wouldn't abuse her trust, and all his cards were on the table. "Especially if you've been in a relationship where you've been taken advantage of."

Erin tilted her head back, lifting her face to his, staring deep into his eyes without a trace of fear or deference. At that moment, she was the least submissive woman he'd ever seen. If he hadn't experienced dominating her himself and seen how she reveled in being controlled, he never would have believed she was the type who enjoyed the lifestyle.

"You don't know anything about my former relationship, and you don't know anything about me," she said, every word clipped and deliberate. "Not anymore. So don't pretend you do. Just because we had sex, it doesn't give you the right to psychoanalyze me. I'm not some pathetic sub who needs someone else to tell me how I'm feeling."

Blake stared into her big brown and gold eyes, seeing so much more than Erin realized. "Is that what he taught you? That to submit is weak and contemptible?"

Without meaning to, he found himself

cupping her cheek in his hand, then sliding his fingers into her impossibly soft hair.

God, how many times had he dreamed of feeling that hair falling around his face as he kissed this woman again? And here she was, so close, but still so incredibly far away.

She was everything he craved, but as forbidden as she'd been years ago when they'd both been too young to realize even true love could vanish in the blink of an eye.

CHAPTER TWO

Blake

Erin's lips parted and her breath came faster, but she didn't say a word. She only watched him, like he was a circus performer about to do some fascinating trick, while Blake prayed he could live up to the expectation in his woman's eyes.

His woman.

There was that thought again, that sense of ownership that felt so natural, but would never be anything but wrong.

"In a real Dominant and submissive relationship, the submissive is an incredibly strong person," he said, hoping she could tell how strong he'd always believed her to be. "Sometimes even stronger than her Dom, depending on how much experience he has."

"Really?" Doubt and sarcasm warred with the genuine curiosity in her tone.

"Just think about it. What requires more discipline, giving someone orders or giving up control?" He leaned closer to her lips, unable to resist. "Trusting someone else to guide you, exploring the boundaries of your capacity for pleasure and pain, giving the gift of your will, of *yourself* to another person…that's pretty amazing stuff. I don't know that I could do it."

"Call me crazy, but I don't think that's your thing." She smiled, a tiny, genuine twist of her lips that made him inexplicably happy.

"Are you calling me a big bad Dom again?" He laughed and she joined in, the puff of her breath against his lips reviving the desire that had haunted him since the second he saw her dancing on that bar in Pasadena.

"I call 'em like I see 'em," she said, tongue slipping out to dampen her lips. "Though I have to admit, I was surprised."

"You and me both. I never thought... Certainly never expected..." Blake took a deep breath and forced himself to pull away. He couldn't stay like this, with his hand buried in her hair and his lips inches from hers, and not take this encounter to the next level.

He stepped back, crossing his arms, concentrating on the feel of the cold wind cutting through the fabric of his sweater. "I want you to know I never planned for there to be anything sexual about this. I expected we'd come up here, have a few beers and a few laughs, I'd modify your tat, and we'd part as friends."

"Or that I would say no to having the tat

modified, you'd hold me captive and modify it whether I liked it or not, and we'd part as enemies," she said, a hint of humor in her tone that made this journey seem even more surreal.

And he hadn't thought it possible.

"I admit that option crossed my mind," he said. "But either way, there wasn't any sex involved. I can promise you that."

"But there definitely is now. So…" She let her words trail off as she stared at him, an unspoken challenge in her eyes that Blake knew he couldn't take her up on. Not if he wanted to keep what was left of his head.

"Don't think I'm not tempted. I'd love to show you what you've been missing," he said, his breath coming faster as he watched her nipples bead tightly beneath her shirt.

Damn, he wanted to get those tits in his mouth and suck them until she writhed beneath him, begging him to take her, fuck her, possess her. But he couldn't.

The first time had been a mistake. A loss of

control that couldn't happen again.

"But I don't think that would be healthy for either one of us," he continued. "We've got a lot of history, Erin. You should have a Dom who can provide for your unique needs and I've got too many of my own."

"Like the driving desire to modify my tattoo," she said, sadness in her eyes.

"Like that." He swallowed the bitter taste that rose in his throat. "And the fact that I've never had a full-time sub and don't plan on getting into something like that any time soon. Especially not with a woman who doesn't seem committed to being a submissive."

She blinked. "Doesn't seem committed? I *lived* it. For years."

He shrugged. "From what I've seen, you're a pushy bottom."

"What?" A ragged laugh burst from her lips.

"From the second we started this, you've been trying to take control. You've questioned and resisted a lot, even for a woman with a new partner," he said, trying to make it clear he wasn't criticizing her, just sharing his opinion. "You try to top from the bottom, and in a real scene, I wouldn't tolerate that. If the woman I'm with wants to be dominated, then that's what I'm going to do. That's who I am. I can't turn it on and off and I wouldn't want to."

She pressed her lips together, a frown tightening the skin around her eyes before she relaxed with a sigh and weary shake of her head. "You know what? Maybe you're right."

His brows crept up his forehead. "Three words a man doesn't hear very often from a woman."

"Even a Dominant man? I'd think you'd get that all the time." She wrapped her arms around herself, shivering as a gust of cold wind blew in the open car door. "But you are. Right, I mean. I'm not sure I'm ready to sub right now. I don't think I'm prepared to make that kind of commitment, even one of the 'fun for a weekend' variety. Especially with a man who cares so little about me that he won't take no for an answer."

"Ouch," he whispered, flinching at the pain in her voice.

So he'd upset her? So what? She'd done her share to upset him in the past. He shouldn't let her emotions affect him so deeply. But they did—he couldn't seem to help himself.

"Let me try to explain again," he said, hoping she'd be able to understand if he opened up and gave her the real reason he needed to banish their matching ink from her skin. "I'll be honest, I was pretty fucked up when you left."

He took a deep breath, wishing it didn't turn him inside out to talk to her this way. But it did. He'd just have to suck it up and get it out as quickly as possible, show he was a true Dom—one as in touch with his own feelings as those of his submissive.

"And I've stayed a little fucked up," he confessed "I loved you like I'd never loved anyone. It hurt to lose you, and looking at this tattoo every day hasn't gotten any easier, especially not when you've used yours as a hook to get modeling work."

"Believe me, Blake, I get it. And I'm sorry this is painful for you." Erin took his hand, her grip strong, though her hand looked almost child-sized compared to his own. "If I didn't really believe I *needed* this tattoo to get work, I would do what you're asking me to do. But I do believe it, and there are other people depending on me and...I just can't risk it. Not now."

"What other people?" he asked, his free hand balling into a fist at his side, itching to defend her before he even knew the facts of her situation. "A boyfriend? Your ex-husband? Is he after you for money?"

"People I don't want to talk about right now," she said, making it clear that was the end of it. "So are you going to take me home or are we going up to this cabin?"

His jaw clenched. "We're going to the cabin."

"Fine," she said, the tightness in her voice making it clear she understood he meant to continue as he'd planned. That he'd modify her tat whether she liked it or not. Still, she took his decision like more of a true submissive than he'd given her credit for.

"Then let's get going, I'm cold." She released his hand and half stood up, climbing into the passenger seat as he opened the driver's door.

Neither of them said a word as he started the car and moved it back onto the road, but Blake made a promise to himself as he drove. He was going to treat Erin with the utmost respect and care, making sure she had nothing to complain about until Sunday afternoon.

Maybe, if he showed her that not all men were pigs and not all Doms bastards who couldn't control their own cock, let alone another's life or pleasure, she would change her mind. Maybe they could get through this together without either of them being hurt.

Of course, that would be more easily

accomplished if he kept his dick in his pants.

Good luck with that, buddy.

Blake gritted his teeth, determined to get control and retain control for the rest of the weekend. He was a man who prided himself on the ability to restrain himself and command others. Surely he could resist giving into temptation.

Especially if he suspected that temptation would get him in even hotter water than he was in already.

CHAPTER THREE

Erin

Erin watched Blake turn onto the narrow road leading up to his cabin with a strange mix of anticipation and dread.

The anticipation, of course, was pretty easy to understand. No matter what Blake had said about a continued sexual relationship being a bad idea, she had no doubt she'd be able to change his mind. He wanted her—badly. It was clear in every heated glance he shot her way, in the tense lines of his body as he guided the car along the twisting mountain roads.

A quickie against the side of his car wasn't going to be enough.

He was going to start jonesing for more than a friendly chat over a few beers and, when that happened, she would be ready to take advantage of the situation. She hadn't had sex in almost two years and she'd never experienced anything close to the pleasure Blake had given her. But that wasn't why she had to risk the emotional fallout that could result from getting too close to this man who still had the ability to affect her like no other. She had to get close to Blake for one reason and one reason only—to gain her freedom.

The man still cared about her. His hurt and longing had been painfully obvious when he'd explained why he needed to modify her tattoo. That care was going to be her ticket out of this cabin with her angel looking exactly the way it had since she was sixteen years old. A little sex, a little submission, and a little conversation between two old friends and Blake would be convinced he had to let her go. He wouldn't be able to force her to do anything if he was falling in love with her again.

And that was where the dread came in.

She'd already hurt him once. What would he do when he found out she had been faking some lovey-dovey act to gain her freedom?

Nothing. Because you'll tell him you'll go to the police.

"We'll be there in a few minutes. You'll want to put your shoes on," Blake said softly, as if he were loathe to break the comfortable silence that had fallen between them.

Erin leaned over and began strapping herself into her heels, ignoring the little thrill obeying even his smallest request gave her.

Blake was wrong. She wasn't a pushy bottom. She lived for the freedom of giving herself to a man who could handle her, and had never had any urge to dominate. She wasn't a switch, she was a sub, through and through. But now wasn't the time or the place and Blake certainly wasn't the man.

It wasn't just her history with Scott that made it hard to let go. Knowing what Blake had in mind for this weekend didn't help matters any. She couldn't afford to abandon herself to him completely, not when the one thing he most wanted to demand of her was something she couldn't give.

The tattoo had to stay looking exactly as it always had if she wanted to get back into modeling for Damned Naughty Lingerie. And she *had* to get back into modeling. Tending bar at The Elbow Room was never going to make her enough money to fight Scott in court, let alone provide for the future. Being a single mother was hard enough, but being a single mother in a city like L.A. was even harder. Everything cost more than it had when she was growing up in a small town, and she was going to need a sizeable income to make sure her daughter Abby never wanted for anything.

Erin didn't want to be dependent on Scott for a dime. She wanted sole custody of their daughter and preferably a restraining order keeping Scott at least ten miles away from them both at all times. Her ex had never hit her or the baby, but he was an emotionally abusive sociopath and the last man who should be entrusted with the care of a child. Especially an infant.

It was enough to make her physically ill every time she thought about Abby going to sleep in the same house as that bastard. She had to get her daughter back, even if it meant fighting the man who had made the past two years of her life a living hell. Even if it meant risking Scott following through with his threats that he would do something awful to Abby before letting her be raised by "a whore like you, Erin."

Erin closed her eyes and swallowed hard,

forcing away the memory of her ex's voice screaming those words as he'd taken Abby away.

She still didn't know how he'd found them. She'd paid the rent for her new apartment in cash, and even given the landlord fake names. But still, Scott had somehow tracked her and their eleven-month-old down and made it very clear the lengths he would go to in order to maintain control over at least one of the girls in his life.

"This is it," Blake said as they turned the last corner and a small cabin came into view. "It's not big, but it's well insulated so we won't freeze our asses off."

He was right, it wasn't big, but even with nothing more than headlights and the porch light to view it by, Erin could see it was gorgeous. Beautiful redwood planks were accented with white trim, making the cabin look like something out of a fairy tale.

"I don't know about that. My ass is already half frozen," Erin said, affecting a light tone.

She had to focus, to stop thinking about Scott and Abby and focus on the immediate problem of getting away from Blake with her tattoo intact. "It would have been nice to know ahead of time I'd be visiting a winter climate. I could have brought my flannel pajamas."

"Hmmm, flannel pajamas. Sounds sexy."

"You have no idea," Erin said, amazed at the tingle of awareness that swept over her skin simply from hearing Blake say the word "sexy." A weekend spent seducing this man certainly wasn't going to be a hardship. "They're bright red with pirates and buried treasure on them. I think they're technically supposed to be for little boys, but as soon as I saw them, I knew they had to be mine."

"I didn't have the creativity to think of something that fasci-smashing," he said, "but I did bring a few things for you to wear."

"Fasci-smashing?" She laughed, a real laugh that surprised her more than it should have. Blake had always been funny in his own, rather dry, way.

"I think it's a cross between fascinating and smashing." He laughed, too, a little self-consciously. "It's something my office manager says all the time. It was added to my vocabulary against my will."

"I don't know what's more disturbing, hearing you say a word like 'fasci-smashing' or learning you brought me clothes." Erin watched Blake closely as he parked the car. "You thought this kidnapping thing through, didn't you?"

He was silent, but Erin deliberately refused to take the hint.

"How long have you been planning to do this?" she pressed.

"A few weeks," he said, all humor vanishing from his tone.

He was embarrassed, she could tell. He knew what he was doing was crazy.

Hopefully that meant getting him to give up on this plan would be relatively easy.

"Should I be freaked out? I mean, have you

turned homicidal maniac on me in the past eight years?" she asked, a part of her thrilled to see Blake's expression grow stormy.

He was wrong about the pushy bottom thing. She didn't want to have control, but she did like to test the man who thought he could top her. When she and Scott had first gotten together, it had been one of the things that he'd loved about her, that she didn't make it easy for him and would only be a good little sub if he was in top form. Though honestly, that wasn't often. Scott hadn't had what it took to master her unless she dialed back the defiance. Still, he'd seemed to treasure their relationship, once upon a time.

But oh, how quickly he'd stopped finding anything lovable about her once she'd gotten pregnant. She'd gone from an object of fascination to a thing of revulsion in less than a few weeks. Long before she'd begun to show, Scott confessed how revolting he found pregnant women, and that he doubted he'd ever be attracted to Erin again.

It was ironic in the extreme, as Erin herself had never felt sexier than when she first found out she was going to have a baby. She'd spent those first few months both unbearably aroused and horribly hurt as she realized her husband no longer wanted anything to do with her—in the bedroom or out of it.

"If you want to press charges against me when we leave," Blake said, his deep voice rumbling through the car's cabin. "I won't do anything to stop you. If that's what you're wondering."

"So you won't kill me and bury my body in the woods?" Erin tried to laugh, but she suddenly wasn't finding the situation funny.

No matter how well she had once known Blake, she didn't know shit about him now. After all, she'd once believed Scott was her Dom in shining black leather, the man she'd be with for the rest of her life. When they'd first married, she couldn't have imagined how quickly her devoted husband would become a monster she despised.

Even if she were right and Blake did still love her, who was to say he didn't have the same capacity for cruelty?

If so, it would certainly prove that she should *never* date again. Her taste in men was decidedly lethal.

"Look at me," Blake said, waiting patiently until she did so. "I would never hurt you. Do you believe I'm telling the truth?"

Erin looked deep into his dark brown eyes, the eyes of the first boy she had ever loved, of the best friend she'd regretted losing for eight years. And for a moment, she was fourteen again—lost and afraid after the foster mom she'd loved so much had died and she'd been placed with a monster. The only way she had survived was by putting on her best tough-girl act and pretending she didn't feel like she was about to shatter into a million pieces. Blake's eyes, and the kind, loving boy they belonged to, were the only things that had gotten her through the day.

No matter what madness had made him

formulate this plan to alter her tattoo, deep down, Blake was still that boy. He would still die before he hurt her, still risk the fists of their foster father or worse to keep her safe. She truly believed that.

"I believe you," Erin whispered, willing the tears she felt pricking at the backs of her eyes not to fall. She wasn't going to cry over old memories. The past was the past. She had to concentrate on the future and her little girl. Nothing else mattered.

"Good." Blake held her gaze, looking near to tears himself, but then a smile spread across his face, making her think she had imagined that moment of vulnerability. "Then let's get inside and I'll find something to cover that frozen ass of yours."

As he exited the vehicle, Erin did her best to pull herself together and figure out the first step in her plan. She believed that Blake didn't want to harm her, but he was still dead set on accomplishing the mission he'd set for himself. And Blake was nothing if not stubborn. It was going to take some intensive persuasive efforts to convince him to change his mind, and she didn't have a lot of time. It was already nearly Saturday morning and she only had until Sunday afternoon.

She was going to have to launch operation Sex Blake Into Forgetting He Owns a Tattoo Gun as soon as possible.

Guess there was no time like the present...

CHAPTER FOUR

Erin

Erin watched Blake walk around the car and grab a large suitcase from the back before she opened her own door and stepped out into the cold night.

"Shit!" She squealed and ran as fast as her high-heeled feet could carry her to the door of the cabin.

It was freezing up on the mountaintop. The wind cut through what few clothes she was wearing, making her feel like she was naked in a snowstorm.

As soon as Blake opened the door to the cabin, she dashed inside, grateful that the heat was already running. If it had been this cold when she and Blake had pulled over for their quickie, even nearly two years without sex wouldn't have been enough to convince her to bang out in the elements.

But it was for the best that they'd broken the ice. He'd already let his guard down and done something he'd freely admitted he hadn't intended to do.

Now it would only take a little push to get them back in bed together.

If the cabin *had* a bed...

"This is gorgeous," Erin said, covertly scanning the small space as Blake went around turning on lights and cranking up the heat.

Just inside the entrance, there was a small

kitchen that opened out into a living area. A comfy-looking sectional filled nearly every inch of the carpet, angled so that it faced both the fireplace in the corner and the floor-to-ceiling windows that looked out across a valley and the dark face of another mountain. It seemed the cabin was built right on the side of a cliff, which would usually have been enough to give her a case of the shakes. She wasn't a big fan of heights, but for some reason she felt safe here.

It was Blake. He had a way of making her feel safe, apparently even when he was the thing she had to be afraid of.

"Thanks. I designed it with the help of a friend of mine." He finished with the lights and came back to fetch the suitcase he'd left by the door. "The bedrooms are upstairs."

Erin followed him, finally noticing the circular staircase that was hidden behind the bathroom to their right. Blake had no trouble navigating the narrow stairs, even with his bulk and carrying a large suitcase, but Erin stumbled twice in her heels. She told herself it was just her normal klutziness coming through, but the truth was, she was nervous.

Touching herself in a dark car or succumbing to maddening lust and leaping out for a quickie on the side of the road was one thing. But starting something from nothing, especially with a man who suddenly seemed all business, was something else entirely.

"Hope you don't mind, but I'm going to give you the smaller room," he said, tossing a friendly smile over his shoulder. "It has a view of the gorge, and you'll have to come through my room if you decide to make a break for it in the middle of the night,"

"And I suppose you still sleep light," she said, finding the situation oddly amusing.

"I wake up if a pinecone drops outside," he said, tramping through a masculine master bedroom, into a bathroom, and through another door to a second bedroom decorated in deep pinks and bright greens.

Those had been her favorite colors in high school, and for a second Erin wondered if Blake had remembered.

"My interior decorator made all the decisions for the furniture and fabrics." He sat the suitcase down on the floral bedspread and opened it. "Hope this isn't too girly for you. I know you're not a big fan of flowers."

"No, it's beautiful," she murmured, pushing aside her childish disappointment that Blake hadn't remembered the preferences of her teenaged self. "It's much nicer than what I've got on the bed at my apartment. Watch out or I might steal the bedspread when we leave."

"You can have it," he said, turning to her with a serious expression. "You can have the entire cabin and the fifteen grand I've got in the glove compartment. All I want to do is work on that tat."

Erin sighed, tempted for a moment. Fifteen grand would pay for a lot of legal advice and having a rent-free place to live would certainly jump-start her and Abby's new life. But for some reason she couldn't bring herself to take Blake up on his offer. She'd meant what she'd said in the car—she believed the tattoo was vital to resuscitating her flagging career—but there was more to her reluctance than that.

The tattoo meant something to her, always had and always would. It reminded her of a time when she'd felt truly loved, like the most important thing in the world to one boy.

"Come on, Erin," Blake urged as if sensing her hesitation. "Don't make me use force."

"But you're a Dom, right?" she teased. "Don't you enjoy using force?"

It was now or never, time to get Blake thinking about her skin in a way that had nothing to do with ink. Holding his dark eyes, she moved her hands to her shirt, slowly working open the buttons, one by one.

"What are you doing?" His tone was casual, but his shoulders tensed as he stepped away from the suitcase.

"I like force," she continued playfully. "If

it's used properly." She slid the shirt off her shoulders, letting it fall to the floor as she began working on the front of her bra, her own excitement building so fast it made her head swim.

Damn. She was going to have to be careful or she was going to get in way over her head.

She parted the bra, baring her breasts to Blake's hungry gaze. "I like to be forcibly restrained, for example."

"Erin," he said, her name a warning. "Stop."

"I like to be forced over a man's knee and spanked." Her hands shook as she worked the button and zipper on her skirt, fresh heat rushing onto her panties as she moved. Just thinking about being turned over Blake's knee, feeling his strong hands reddening her ass, his fingers slipping between her legs to see how wet his punishment had made her, made her entire body ache.

"I'll tell you one more time," he rumbled. "Stop. Or there will be consequences for disobeying me."

Wow. He'd whipped out the silky Dom voice, so deep and commanding, promising retribution. It was nearly enough to make her come without him laying a finger on her.

"I like to feel a hand fisting in my hair," she continued in a breathy voice, not bothering to hide her arousal, "forcing my head back as I get fucked from—"

He moved so quickly that, afterward, Erin didn't remember seeing him close the distance between them. He was simply across the room one minute and slamming her into the wall the next, every inch of his hard body pressed tightly against hers, his lips claiming her mouth in a bruising kiss that made her bones melt.

Oh. Hell. Yeah.

Looked like they wouldn't be making it to the bed after all, but Erin wasn't going to complain. *This* was exactly the way she wanted the night to end. In Blake's arms, getting ready for a second helping of the kind of pleasure she knew she'd never get enough of.

But you will get enough.

And then you'll get the hell away from him and get your life back on track.

The voice of reason. What a pale, sad little thing it was when a man like Blake was slipping his hand between her legs, shoving his fingers up and inside where she was already desperate for him to be.

CHAPTER FIVE

Blake

Blake's tongue pushed inside Erin's mouth, demanding entrance, claiming her with firm strokes of his tongue against hers while his fingers teased in and out of her pussy. She tasted as amazing as she always had, like summer wind and the ocean they'd dreamed of seeing together and something all Erin that made him feel the kiss with his entire self—body and soul.

Kissing Erin was nearly as intimate as fucking her. She communicated things with those lips, teeth, and tongue that were beyond words. Mating his mouth with hers had always felt like they were rubbing souls, sharing dreams, devouring a little piece of each other with every press of their lips. In the old days, all the things they were too young or afraid to tell each other aloud had been said in those hours spent making out in the backseat of his Impala.

Just kissing, not taking things much further, neither of them willing to risk that the perfection of those stolen moments would be destroyed by going too far too fast.

"Blake." She moaned his name into his mouth, her desire clear. Her fingers dug into his shoulders, silently imploring him to get closer and shove something more serious than his fingers between her legs.

"Do you want me to fuck you again, Erin?"

he asked, moving his thumb to her clit as his fingers continued to drive inside her molten heat with slow, even strokes.

"Do you have to ask?" She hooked one leg around his hips, granting him better access to her pussy.

"No." He slipped a third finger inside her, drawing another moan from the woman in his arms. The sound vibrated against his lips, making his head spin. "But I'd still like an answer."

"Yes. God, yes. Please." She bucked into his hand, sheathing his digits inside her again and again. "I want you."

"How much?" he asked, feeling how close she was to the edge by the way her cunt gripped his fingers. She was nearly irresistible when she was like this, so abandoned, so desperate for her pleasure.

But he was going to have to resist. If he couldn't stay the hell away from Erin, he'd have to do the next best thing—show her who was in control. It was what she secretly craved, any Dom with the sense God gave a donut could see that. More important, it was what he had to do. He *had* to show her he meant business, in the bedroom and out, and that this weekend would be proceeding as he had planned. He had to ensure she would do what he told her and stop fighting him at every turn.

What happened to being Mr. Nice Guy?

Fuck Mr. Nice Guy.

He'd be Mr. Nice Dom, it was a role that suited him better.

"Tell me, Erin. How much do you want me to fuck you?" he asked again, finally getting an answer when he withdrew his hand from between her legs.

"More than anything," she said, with a sob, making it clear how much she lamented the loss of his touch.

"Show me." Blake pulled away from her addictive lips, ignoring the tremor that rocked through both of them at the loss of contact. Breaking off a kiss with Erin already felt like breaking off a piece of himself.

All the more reason to get them back on the right track—the track to mutual pleasure, not the one feeding his foolish infatuation.

With his hands firmly on her shoulders, Blake urged Erin to the ground in front him. There was a question in her eyes, but she held her tongue as she sank to her knees at his feet.

"I want you to take care of something for me before I take care of you." He opened the button of his fly and drew down the zipper, tugging his jeans and boxer briefs lower on his hips, freeing his turgid length.

His cock was already as hard as if they'd been at their make-out session for a few hours, not a few minutes. All nine inches were thick and aching, the head nearly purple from the amount of blood rushing to his groin. It was amazing he still had enough blood flowing to his brain to form words, let alone exercise the restraint it took to wait as Erin devoured him with her eyes.

The lust on her face made him crazy, and

the tip of her pink tongue sweeping over her top lip made him even crazier. She looked like she couldn't wait to get his cock in her mouth, to suck him between those full lips and show him what he'd been missing in the eight years away from her.

But she didn't reach out to capture his length in her hands, or lean forward to take him into her mouth. She simply knelt at his feet, waiting for him to tell her what to do, showing she wasn't nearly as inexperienced as he'd suspected. In fact, submissive behavior seemed to come naturally to her. It was the other stuff that was forced—the defiance, the testing the limits of the man who would dominate her.

A bad habit learned from living with a man who couldn't handle her, no doubt. Good thing Blake was certain he was twice the Dom her ex-husband had been, or he might have been nervous himself. Erin wasn't an easy woman to top. He was going to have to earn every last ounce of submission he coaxed from the woman at his feet.

It was an intoxicating experience. One he feared might ruin him for other women and the scenes he'd enjoyed up until now.

How could he go back to those silly girls who hit the BDSM clubs once a week to play when he'd had a chance to test the boundaries of a woman like Erin?

"Do you want me to take you in my mouth?" she asked, licking her lips again, the sight making a pearl of pre-cum leak from the tip of Blake's cock.

"Yes," Blake said, his voice deeper, rougher.

"With pleasure, sir." A naughty smile flitted across her face as she leaned forward, pausing only centimeters away from his swollen tip.

Slowly she rolled her eyes up to meet his and parted her lips, letting her breath warm his eager flesh for one second, then two, before finally taking the plumped head of his cock into the wet heat of her mouth. Blake did his best not to groan as she lingered there, suckling him, running her teeth lightly over the ridge, where head became shaft.

For what seemed like hours she played with him, pulling just his tip between her lips then moving away, running her tongue around and around the slit at the end of his cock until he genuinely began to leak. But even then she didn't intensify her efforts, she only moaned and lapped away the evidence of his need as if she couldn't get enough of the taste of his cum on her tongue.

If that was the case, he was going to give her more of what she was craving. Very soon. But he'd prefer it to be *after* he'd fucked that pretty mouth the way it deserved to be fucked.

Gritting his teeth, Blake reached down, threading his fingers into Erin's hair. He caressed her gently, sliding his fingers through the blond silk, marveling that anything could feel so soft. Only when he felt the muscles in her neck relax did he fist his hand, claiming control of her in one swift movement.

Erin sucked in a swift breath, surprise and lust mingling in the small sound.

Blake looked down into her eyes, holding them as he tightened his grip in her hair. Then, without a word of warning, he tugged her forward, plunging into her wet mouth.

His cock disappeared between her lips and all too soon he hit the back of her throat. He paused, giving her time to adjust, to relax the muscles barring his deeper penetration. Then he thrust deeper, and deeper still, forcing her to take over half of his length. Once he was there, buried as deeply as he thought she could handle, he held still, studying her face.

Her eyes squeezed closed and she seemed to struggle to accommodate him, but only for a moment. Soon her breath was coming faster, in and out of her nose in swift bursts that warmed the top of his shaft. Her breasts rose and fell as she suckled him, her nipples pebbling tight and her hips shifting back and forth. Her mounting desire was obvious, so obvious he wasn't surprised when she slipped a hand between her legs, clearly intending to take care of herself with her fingers while her mouth was busy with his cock.

"No, Erin. Don't touch my pussy." Blake pulled away before thrusting swiftly back inside her, demanding her attention. "You can play with your tits if you want, but don't touch my pussy."

He'd done it again, but this time Blake didn't regret claiming her pussy as his own. He wasn't going to fight something that felt so right.

For the next two days, she would belong to him, every last part of her, from those hazel eyes to that sweet little pussy he was going to teach another valuable lesson about delayed gratification.

But first, he was going to enjoy some gratification of his own.

CHAPTER SIX

Blake

For the next few minutes, the world disappeared. There were no thoughts of Erin's tattoo, there was no stress about what this weekend would hold for the two of them, there was no worry about the wisdom of indulging in Dom-sub play with the least suitable woman he could have chosen.

There was only Erin.

Erin's mouth, hot and eager, sucking him impossibly farther inside her wet heat. Her tongue rolling against his engorged cock, her hands sliding around to cup his ass, fingernails digging into the muscled flesh until he groaned. Her little moans as he fucked her mouth, the hint of tears glistening in her eyes as his penetration grew more intense, the silent urging of her hands on his buttocks, telling him not to back off, not to stop until he was shooting himself between her lips.

Finally, the combined stimulation was too much. A deep cry ripped from his chest as he came, his cock jerking inside her mouth, cum gushing from his body in thick, hot jets.

"God, Erin," he said, his voice hoarse with desire as he watched her jaw work. She swallowed him down, milking his cock dry with a look of such bliss he knew he would have been hard again immediately if nature had allowed it.

After a few moments, she pulled away,

slowly, letting his cock slip from between her lips with obvious regret. Only then did she lift her eyes to his, a new question in their expressive depths.

"The best blow job of my life. Bar none, beautiful." Blake's hand softened in her hair, then moved down to cup her cheek. God, she was lovely. He let his fingers trail down her jaw to her chin before pulling away to tuck himself back in his pants. "What do you want now, baby?"

"Whatever you want," she said, her breath coming fast, her brow furrowing as she watched him put away his cock. She clearly wasn't happy to see it go, which pleased him more than it should have.

"Are you sure about that?" he asked. "You're ready to give me whatever I want? No holds barred?"

"Yes." She lifted her eyes to his once more, the hunger he read in their depths making him shiver.

Her breasts were as flushed as her cheeks

and her nipples were so tight Blake knew they had to be aching uncomfortably. She'd been genuinely turned on by what she'd done to him, a fact that blew him away. It was a rare woman who got off on giving a blow job.

But then, a true submissive got off on anything that gave her lover pleasure. As did a true Dom, for that matter.

Unfortunately, what gave a submissive pleasure could be a little more complicated.

"Good. Because I'm going to fuck you," Blake said, holding her gaze, feeling his cock thicken as her breath shuddered out from between her lips. "I'm going to eat your wet pussy, and then I'm going to fuck you until you scream. First your pussy and then your ass if I decide that's what I'd like. Would you want me to fuck your ass, Erin?"

"I want you to fuck me everywhere." Erin's breath came faster and her hands balled into fists at her sides.

He could tell it was getting harder for her to wait, to keep from reaching for what she wanted. For a moment, it almost made him rethink his plan. But then, the fact that she was nearing the edge of her control was all the more reason to test it.

"Good girl. Then I'll see you tomorrow morning." He turned back toward the suitcase on the bed, but not before he saw the shocked expression on Erin's face. "I promise it will be worth the wait."

"Tomorrow morning?" she asked, her tone leaving no doubt how frustrating she found the thought of delaying her gratification. "You can't be serious."

Blake smiled as he pulled out a pair of white cotton panties and a green sleep shirt from the clothes he'd packed for Erin, but he was careful to banish the grin from his face before he turned back to her. "I am. I'm going downstairs to take a shower." He calmly held out the clothes. "You're welcome to shower up here at the same time. There's plenty of hot water."

"Plenty of hot water?" She laughed, a short,

abrupt sound.

"There's soap, shampoo, and conditioner in the cabinet and a new toothbrush and toothpaste in the drawer." He zipped the suitcase shut and picked it up, realizing that if Erin decided to run, it would be best if he didn't give her access to the winter clothes he'd brought.

Of course, in her present state of mind, she might decide it was a good idea to run out into the snow in nothing but her nightshirt and bare feet.

Just in case he added—

"We're about ten miles from the nearest cabin. I wouldn't try to run if I were you."

"You're not going to just leave me like this, are you?" she blinked wide, pained eyes, gesturing down at herself as if her state of arousal should be abundantly obvious.

And it was. *Damn*, it was.

Her skin was flushed all over and her tits were so swollen, he could only imagine how swollen and wet her pussy must be, and how fucking good she would taste as he plunged his tongue inside her.

It wasn't easy to resist crossing the room, kneeling in front of her, and taking her nipples in his mouth. He could almost feel how perfectly they would stiffen beneath his tongue, hear how she'd moan as he coaxed her into a state of even more powerful lust. They probably wouldn't even make it to the bed. He'd end up taking her there on the floor, her long legs wrapped around his face as he devoured her, making her come screaming his name before he spread her wide and shoved inside her, burying his cock to the hilt in her heat, fucking her until—

Thankfully, Erin spoke before the weakness in his mind could become weakness of the body.

"Blake, please," she begged. "I need you. I swear to God, I'm going to go crazy if you don't touch me."

"I warned you to stop," he said, his tone remarkably calm considering where his thoughts had been heading a moment before. "And I warned you there would be consequences for disobeying."

"This isn't a consequence; it's cruel and unusual punishment," she said, but even with the angry, frustrated look on her face, he could tell being disciplined excited her.

"I'll take care of you in the morning. Sleep well." He crossed the room, toting the suitcase with him to the door, where he paused to look back at Erin one more time. "And don't think about using that detachable nozzle in the shower or your hand or anything else, beautiful. I'll know if you don't wait for me to make you come, and I won't be happy."

"Maybe I don't care if you're happy," she mumbled beneath her breath, but he heard every word, like she'd wanted him to.

In a matter of seconds, he'd dropped the suitcase and was by her side, pushing her back onto the carpet. He stretched out on top of her, spreading her legs with a rough nudge of his knee, grinding his erection against her through their clothes. Her lips met his with a cry and her hands shook as she looped them around his neck. He kissed her, softly, insistently, thoroughly, until she was bucking against his cock, and her breath came in desperate pants.

Only then did he pull away to look deep into her eyes.

"If you really don't care if I'm happy, or pleased with you, then we should stop this right now," he said, his voice low and firm. "A submissive takes pleasure from being obedient, it's the definition of the word. So if obeying me doesn't give you pleasure, if it isn't a gratifying thing in its own right, then I don't see how this can work between us."

"I'm sorry," she said, the vulnerable note in her voice causing some of the tension to seep from his body, making him even more aware of all the places they touched. "This is just so confusing. Things didn't use to be this way between us. I keep thinking about when we were in high school and..." Her teeth dug into her bottom lip as she pulled in a shaky breath. "It feels like I'm caught between two different versions of myself and I don't know which one to be. If that makes any sense?"

"It does," he said, smoothing her hair from her forehead. "But I can't be anyone but the man I am now. Maintaining control is part of who I am, the way I prove to myself that I'm not like the foster fathers I was stuck with when I was a kid. If we're going to give each other pleasure, I need you to trust and respect me. To want to obey me because that's what's going to get you off the hardest."

"I do," she said, pain flashing in her eyes. "I just want you so much. It will be so hard to wait."

Warmth spread through his chest. "I know. Believe me, beautiful, it's not going to be easy for me, either. I've been dying to get my mouth between your legs since the moment I saw you tonight." He leaned down, pressing a soft kiss to the tip of her nose. "But I promise you, if you trust me, I'll make it worth your while."

She took a deep breath, letting it out slowly as her arms slipped away from his neck. "First thing tomorrow morning?"

"I'll have your pussy for breakfast. I swear." He kissed her one last time, relishing the way her moan of anticipation buzzed against his lips before he pulled back and came to his feet.

Blake strode to the door, grabbed the suitcase, and started downstairs without turning to look over his shoulder. If he had and he'd been forced to see Erin sprawled nude on the carpet, that come-hither look in her eyes, he wasn't sure he would have had the strength to leave.

Some Dom he was.

But then, he hadn't been prepared to exert the kind of control it took to top a girl like Erin. He'd never dreamed she'd summon not only the intense, undeniable chemistry they'd shared as teenagers but also stimulate the very adult desires he'd acquired since then.

He'd finally met his match, the kind of woman he could see himself playing with for years, the strong yet submissive partner he hadn't dreamed he'd find.

Too bad she was also the woman who had broken his heart and a person who couldn't be trusted.

He had never guessed she was planning to leave Carson City the morning after they swore to spend their lives together and sealed the promise with a pair of matching tattoos. There hadn't been the slightest sign. Hell, they'd made love right after he'd finished the work on her shoulder, sneaking into the camper behind their friend Kevin's house to do it in a bed instead of his car for a change. Even at eighteen, Blake had known he'd never forget that night, how beautiful Erin had looked as she rode him, and how excited he'd felt knowing he was soon going to be in control of his own life.

He'd had a job lined up as a bouncer at a local bar and was working part-time with the best tattoo artist in town. In a few months, he'd expected to have the portfolio and the money he needed to make the move to Reno, and from there, eventually on to Vegas. Erin was going to get her GED and go with him. They'd had it all planned out.

But then she'd run away, without leaving so much as a note to tell him why. Blake hadn't even realized she was gone until he'd shown up at Casa de la Hell looking for her and Phil had tried to kick his ass.

"Where is she?" Phil came at him with fists raised. "Where's Erin? And where's my goddamned truck, you son of a bitch."

Blake was so shocked—and so busy putting two and two together to make one gone girl—that he didn't lift his arms in time. Phil's first punch connected with his jaw and Blake fell to the ground, his ears ringing. But he was back on his feet in seconds, charging Phil with a roar born of the fear and rage pumping through his bloodstream.

Erin was gone.

She'd taken Phil's truck and run, the way she'd

threatened to do a hundred times before. But this time she'd really done it. She'd run away and left him behind, right when they were about to have everything they'd been dreaming about for years.

Blake took Phil to the ground and pounded on the bastard's face until his former foster father begged him to let him go, but it didn't bring Erin back. And it didn't make Blake feel better.

Nothing made him feel better, not for a very, very long time.

The sound of the water turning on upstairs jolted Blake back to the present, making him wonder how long he'd been standing at the bottom of the stairs with a death grip on the handle of the suitcase and bad memories souring the taste of Erin's kiss.

"Too long," he mumbled aloud.

Any time spent dwelling on those old memories was too much time. He'd already learned the lessons he needed from those days. He'd learned not to trust Erin, no matter how much he'd loved her.

No matter how much he was beginning to

think he *still* loved her, he'd be a fool to forget she was the kind of woman who would make you think you were the center of her universe one minute.

And the next minute, she'd be gone.

LILI VALENTE

CHAPTER SEVEN

Erin

"I'll take care of you in the morning." Erin mimicked Blake's bossy voice as she scrubbed her skin with the loofah until it stung, struggling to ignore the heavy, swollen feeling in her breasts and that way her pussy ached with a need that was physically painful.

Damnit! She'd never felt so dissatisfied, not

even after what Blake had ordered her to do in the car.

Every nerve ending in her body screamed for relief from the unfulfilled desire coursing through her veins and her breath came in angry little pants. Dom or not, Blake had no right to do this to her, especially not twice in one night. She hadn't been *that* defiant, and she had blown him like it was her sole mission on earth.

Blown him…

God help her, but even the memory of it was enough to make her pussy wetter. Blake's was the first cock she'd ever seen and it was still her favorite. The thing was just fucking beautiful—long and thick, with a bulbous head that filled her mouth like a perfectly shaped plum. And it wasn't just pretty, but made for a woman's pleasure. The thick ridge between the head and shaft rubbed all the right places, stretching her, filling her, until there was nothing but Blake. Nothing but pleasure—raw, hot, and wild.

Erin growled through gritted teeth, throwing the loofah to the shower floor in frustration.

Take care of her in the morning, her ass. She'd take care of herself. Right now. There was no way she'd be able to sleep if she didn't ease the tension making her teeth itch and her skin crawl with frustration.

Erin pulled the shower nozzle from its place on the wall, a thrill of excitement shooting through her as she used it to wash the last of the soap from her body. It wasn't just the fact that she was getting ready to come that thrilled her; it was the knowledge that she was defying Blake, disobeying a direct order.

Maybe he was right, and she was a naughty sub who needed to be punished, but that wasn't going to stop her. She needed to take the edge off before she lost what was left of her mind.

Sticking her head out of the shower curtain for a moment, Erin listened carefully.

Thankfully, she could still hear the water running downstairs. Blake wasn't finished with his shower, which meant he wouldn't be coming to check on her for at least a few minutes.

"A few minutes is all it will take." Erin sighed in relief as she lay down in the tub, propping one foot on the side, baring the needy place between her legs. Moving one hand to her breast, she plucked at her already erect nipple, building the fire smoldering within her to near the breaking point. Then, with shaking hands, she moved the shower nozzle between her legs.

Erin gasped as the water streamed over her clit. God, she was so close…so fucking close. Just a few more seconds, just a little more pressure and then…

Then…

"Please, please," she moaned softly, her breath rasping in and out as she pinched her nipples and squirmed beneath the warm spray coursing between her legs. But her pleasure never crested and the tension building inside stayed just south of the breaking point.

Fuck! What was wrong with her? She'd never had a problem bringing herself over. Usually in less than sixty seconds.

When you lived under the thumb of a domineering man who refused to have sex with you, but had forbidden you to pleasure yourself, you learned to get the job done as quickly as possible. If she hadn't been adept at getting herself off, she probably would have lost her mind during the past two years.

So why was her body failing her now?

And don't think about using that detachable nozzle in the shower or your hand or anything else. I'll know if you don't wait for me and I won't be happy.

Blake's words echoed through her head. A moment later, Erin's eyes slid closed with a curse. Her arm went limp, the showerhead sliding down to pelt water against her thigh.

No matter what the rational part of her thought about the games she and Blake were playing, it seemed her body had decided

Blake's happiness was essential. It wasn't going to let her come because it didn't want to displease the man downstairs.

Apparently, her good little submissive act hadn't been as much of an act as she'd thought. And now she was going to have to wait until morning for relief. Her twisted libido wouldn't allow her to do anything else.

The realization was enough to bring tears to her eyes.

This wasn't the first time she'd wished she'd never started exploring this side of herself, never admitted she craved the act of submission. The highs were admittedly very high, but the lows of the past two years should have taught her the danger in walking this path.

She needed to be in control right now. She had to concentrate on getting her life back on track, not on servicing another man. Even if this was only for a weekend, it wasn't smart.

Hell, if her head had already decided obeying Blake was *necessary* in order to claim her own pleasure, this was downright dangerous.

Tears of fear and frustration flowed down her cheeks as she finished her shower and dried off. She pulled on the panties and nightshirt Blake had brought for her, but even the soft fabric felt abrasive against her sensitized skin. She brushed her hair with swift, rough strokes, and, after a little searching, found the toothbrush and toothpaste.

She'd just finished rinsing her mouth when footsteps sounded on the stairs, making her hurry to complete her nighttime routine and escape to the relative safety of her bedroom.

If she had to see Blake again or smell the addictive scent of the man she loved, she'd—

"No. No, no, no." Erin chanted the mantra under her breath as she dashed to the bed, snapped off the bedside lamp, and curled into a ball beneath the covers.

She *wasn't* falling in love with Blake again. It was impossible. They'd only been back together for a night and no amount of hot sex could make up for quality time spent learning to care for each other again.

Unless, of course, she had never *stopped* loving him in the first place.

Erin moaned softly into the luxurious pillowcase, fresh tears slipping down her cheeks, though the reason for them wasn't completely clear.

Was she crying for herself, or for Blake? For what they'd lost, or for what they'd never have again, no matter how hot the chemistry was between them?

She didn't know.

There were many things in life that confused her, but love had always been the biggest and most confusing thing of all.

CHAPTER EIGHT

Erin

When Erin woke up the next morning, the room was aglow with soft yellow light and a slightly rumpled Blake was lying beside her, propped up on one elbow, watching her sleep. Even before she'd had a chance to shake off the sleep cobwebs, the tender expression on his face brought her fears from the night before rushing back with a vengeance.

The surge of anxiety was strong enough to make her scoot a few inches away, despite the fact that the heat rolling from Blake's body made her long to curl into his chest and go right back to sleep.

Great, now she was craving snuggling in addition to sex. If that wasn't a sign that she was treading dangerous waters, she didn't know what was.

"Good morning," Blake said, his deep voice vibrating across her skin, making her nipples tighten. "Did you sleep well?"

"Pretty well," she said. "Considering I was dying of frustration when I went to sleep."

"I'm glad you kept your promise," he said. "I'd hate to have to neglect your pussy any longer." A smile pulled at the corners of his full lips, making her want to smile along with him. Blake could be scary-looking when he wanted to be, but when he smiled he was simply...beautiful.

"What are you thinking?" he asked, smile

fading.

"That you're beautiful," she said, unable to lie when he was looking at her like she was all he needed in the whole world to be happy.

"Not half as beautiful as you are." His eyes darkened as he reached out, twisting a strand of her hair around his finger. "I'd forgotten it was curly when you don't use that thing on it."

"It's called a flattening iron. You bought me one for Christmas sophomore year, remember?"

Erin knew she should keep her thoughts in the present and her interactions with Blake purely physical, but she couldn't seem to resist a trip down memory lane. It had been so long since anyone had looked at her the way he was looking at her now, with need and affection mixing in his features.

Foolish or not, she craved the warmth in his expression almost as much as she craved his body.

"I forgot what it was called," he said with a

crooked grin. "You're the only girlfriend I ever lived with, and you know we didn't spend much time getting ready at home."

"Yeah, six people sharing one bathroom was fun." Erin shuddered as she remembered Phil's Pepto-Bismol-colored toilet and the tub with the cracks up the side. She'd shared the festering lav with Blake, Phil, his wife, and an endlessly shifting group of younger foster kids.

Erin had tried not to remember their names or faces. It was easier that way. If she didn't get attached, she didn't have to freak out when they went to school with bruises hidden beneath their clothes or without breakfast in their bellies because Phil had gone on a bender and they didn't have money left over to buy cereal or milk.

"It was easier to get ready at school." She closed her eyes and rubbed at the tops, wishing she could wipe away the visions of the sad little faces conjured by her thoughts.

"Yeah," Blake agreed. "Or in Kevin's

camper."

Erin's eyes slit open as she sneaked a peek at Blake's face. She wondered if he remembered that Kevin's camper was where they'd spent their last night together. But Blake's features were calm, impassive. He didn't seem to make the connection. Of course, he hadn't known it was their last night. She hadn't wanted to ruin it for him by telling him their plan was never going to work, not while she was still underage.

There was no way she could have kept living in Casa de la Hell without Blake, and no way Phil would have let a sixteen-year-old minor in his "care" move out to live with her boyfriend. She'd felt like she had no choice but to get out of town, *way* out of town, and make sure Blake wouldn't be blamed for her disappearance. It was the best thing she could do for him at the time, the only gift she had to give.

"You hungry?" he asked, releasing the curl he'd wrapped around his finger. "I've got the stuff to make waffles downstairs. And bacon and eggs, or yogurt, if you want something lighter."

"You know me, the more food, the better. I still have trouble keeping on weight. Even when I was—" Erin broke off, biting her lip. "Even when I'm getting to the gym as much as I should."

Shit! She'd nearly mentioned her pregnancy. She didn't want Blake to know she had a daughter, or that she'd screwed things up so royally right out of the gate. He'd either hate her for letting Scott take Abby—they'd always sworn they would protect their kids if they had any of their own—or he'd decide to go wring Scott's neck with his bare hands.

As appealing as that image was, Erin didn't want to be responsible for getting Blake put in jail. And she didn't want him to feel obligated to help rescue her from the mess she was in, either. She already had a plan in place to rescue herself. She had some money saved and an appointment with the marketing head of Damned Naughty Lingerie next Friday.

Kelsey Greer had always been a big "Angel" fan. She was certain he'd hire her on for the spring catalog photo shoot. Maybe not in her former position as the "it girl," but the job would still earn her a few grand. Then she'd be in a much better position to keep Abby safe while she fought Scott in court.

Or you could take that fifteen grand Blake's offering and be in an even better place, even sooner.

Erin bit the inside of her cheek, ignoring the voice of temptation. She didn't want Blake's money, especially not for letting him alter her tattoo. Even if she could convince herself that a slightly different fallen angel would serve her modeling career as well as the one she had, she didn't want to look over her shoulder in the mirror and see anything but what she saw now.

That ink had kept her connected to Blake, no matter how much time and distance had separated them. It had given her comfort in some of her hardest moments, that evidence that she had once been so special to another person.

It was obvious Blake was more crazed than comforted by their matching tats, but she still couldn't imagine having that part of their past wiped away. Losing this tat would be like losing a piece of herself, her last connection to the girl she'd been and the boy she'd loved so much she'd had no choice but to leave him behind.

"So I guess that's a yes for breakfast?" Blake asked, breaking into her thoughts.

"Yeah." Erin ignored the tightness in her chest. "Breakfast sounds good."

Blake cupped her face in his big hand. "What's wrong?"

"Nothing." She smiled, determined not to get her feelings hurt by the fact that Blake wanted to erase the evidence of their past.

She'd known that's what he wanted since last night. Why should it bother her so much more this morning?

Because now you know you still love him, that you

never stopped loving him.

"I'm starving, let's eat." She tried to sit up, but a rock-hard arm closed around her waist, pinning her to the covers.

"I haven't forgotten my promise," Blake said, his hand wandering down to her bare thigh, caressing her with a gentle insistence that had her body waking up faster than a double shot of espresso. "I just wanted to make sure I wasn't starving you. You can't live on love alone."

"Lust alone, you mean," Erin said, but the joke fell flat, and Blake's brow furrowed in response.

He looked almost hurt by the correction.

Could he be feeling the same way she did? The way he had when they were so young and stupid, but so very much in love?

The thought should have been exhilarating. Less than eight hours ago she'd sworn to do whatever it took to make Blake fall for her again, and then use his feelings to make the weekend end the way she wanted it to end.

But now, the thought of Blake loving her just hurt.

It hurt so bad she couldn't keep her face from crumpling or tears from rising in her eyes.

CHAPTER NINE

Erin

"Babe, don't cry. What's wrong?" Blake pulled his hand away from her thigh, surrounding her with his arms and pulling her close to his chest.

He was so much bigger and stronger than he'd been when they were younger, but the feeling of safety that coursed through her when he held her was still the same.

God, why had she ever left him?

No matter how bad things had been at her foster home, she should have stayed and found a way to wait for him.

How had she ever thought she'd be okay without Blake?

Of course, at sixteen, she hadn't realized how precious he was. She'd known there weren't a lot of good guys out there, but deep down, she'd assumed she would find another man to give her heart to and move on from her first love. But she hadn't moved on, not even when things were good with Scott. She'd never loved her husband the way she loved Blake. And on those nights when she knew her marriage was beyond redemption and she'd cried herself to sleep, it wasn't Scott's arms she imagined holding her close, making her feel safe and loved.

It was Blake. It had always been Blake. And it probably always would be.

But that didn't change anything. Blake

didn't want her, not really. If he did, he
wouldn't have written asking her to change
her tattoo. He would have written asking to
see her again, to see if they could reconnect,
go back, or at least start over. He hadn't
known she was married. She'd kept her
maiden name. Erin Perry was the name she
was known for and certainly sounded more
like it belonged to a lingerie model than Erin
Sakapatatis.

No, Blake didn't want her back. He was
clearly up for a weekend fling, but what Blake
truly wanted was his freedom. Whatever it
was he still felt for her, he wanted those
feelings gone, and he thought modifying her
tattoo was the way to make that happen.

Who knew, maybe it was. Maybe the
connection between them would finally be
severed when they no longer sported
matching ink.

The thought made her sadder than she'd
been since the day Scott walked out of her
apartment with her baby in his arms.

"I'm okay." She sniffed, wishing she had a Kleenex. Seconds later, Blake plucked one from the bedside table and pressed it into her hand, reading her mind again, the way he always did.

The small act of compassion was nearly enough to get her tears going again, but she pressed her lips together, fighting for control.

"Listen, I meant what I said," Blake murmured in that deep, sexy voice of his. "I don't want to hurt you, and I really don't want to make you cry."

"I know." Erin wiped her nose, breath rushing out when she glanced up to see Blake's eyes tight around the edges. "You look scared."

"A crying woman is a scary thing." He tucked a stray lock of hair behind her ear. "Especially you. I can count the times I've seen you cry on one finger."

"Yeah, I guess you're right. I wasn't much of a crier back in the day." She sighed, remembering the tough nut she used to be.

Of course, it had only been a smokescreen, a front to hide how scared and sad she truly was. Her years in Carson City had been fraught with fear, every minute lived under a dark shadow, except those moments when she and Blake would steal away and escape into their own world.

"It's all right," she said, swiping the tears from her cheeks with her fist. "I cry all the time now. It's no big deal."

"Sounds like a big deal to me." His brow furrowed. "What's been making you cry? Your ex?"

"Let's not talk about my ex," Erin said, tossing her Kleenex to the floor behind her. "In fact, let's not talk at all."

Before Blake could say a word, she wrapped her arms around his neck and pulled him down for a kiss. And then another kiss and another until he groaned into her mouth and rolled on top of her, crushing her into the mattress with his weight.

Slowly, all her fears and worries vanished in

the wake of the heat that flared between them. Erin wrapped her legs around his hips, a moan bursting from her lips when she felt how hard he was beneath his blue-and-white-striped pajama bottoms.

He captured her bottom lip, suckling it deeper into his mouth, raking his teeth over the sensitive skin as he pulled away. Her breath rushed out and her nipples pulled tight. She'd never realized she enjoyed being bitten so much. But she enjoyed everything Blake did to her, even the stuff she was sure she hated.

Like it or not, he'd been right to make her wait. She was even more eager to have him now than she'd been last night, and when she finally came, she knew it was going to blow her mind. And probably her heart, too, but she wasn't going to think about that now.

She wasn't going to think about anything except how amazing Blake made her feel.

"I can't believe we're still in our pajamas with the sun that high in the sky," she said, reaching down to run her fingers under the waistband of his pants. "I think it's time we got out of them."

"I couldn't agree more," he rumbled against her lips, making them tingle.

Soon, they were pulling at each other's clothes, breath coming faster as shirts and pants were tossed aside and sighing as their bodies came back together with nothing to separate skin from skin. And for a moment, as her breasts pressed against Blake's hard, lightly furred chest and her lips met his— teeth bumping together as they kissed with enough passion to set the world on fire—Erin felt safe and happy.

As safe and happy as she'd always felt with the only man she'd ever truly loved.

CHAPTER TEN

Blake

Blake pulled away from Erin, looking down at where she lay naked beneath him, her hair glowing gold in the morning light. She'd washed off the makeup she'd had on last night and looked the way she had eight years ago. Even the look in her eyes was the same, that raw, vulnerable, needy look that had always made him feel like the focus of her entire world—at least for the moment.

She was a ghost come back to haunt him and it would have been enough to make his heart ache if he'd let it. But he wasn't dwelling on past losses or betrayals now, not when he was about to fuck the most beautiful woman he'd ever seen.

And not when, unexpectedly, he felt happier and more content than he had in years.

"I want to eat my pussy," Blake said, running his hands up and down her soft thighs, his cock pulsing hungrily between his legs.

"Are you sure?" She wiggled her hips, grinding her center against his erection, her breath coming in sexy little pants that drove him crazy. "Are you sure you don't want to wait? Fuck me now and have your pussy for dessert?" A pained expression flashed across her face. "I want you inside me so bad, Blake. So bad."

"I need to taste you first, sweetness. I was dreaming about getting my tongue inside you all night." He dipped his hand between them, capturing her wetness on his fingertips and bringing them to his lips. He moaned as the intimate flavor of her spread across his tongue.

She tasted as amazing as she ever had—clean and sweet with an edge of salt and a feminine musk that was enough to drive him crazy. To him, the taste of Erin was the taste of pure desire. It was enough to make him even harder, thicker. He shifted his hips, grinding his cock against where she was so wet and ready. It was tempting to forget his plans and drive straight into the sweet pussy he'd been dreaming about since he'd left her last night.

But she'd proven she could keep her promises. Now he was going to prove he could keep his.

He truly was dying to get his mouth on her. He wanted to see if Erin was as responsive as she'd been the last time he'd lowered his head between her legs, and to show her he'd learned a thing or two about giving a woman pleasure since his eighteenth birthday.

"Open your legs. Spread them wide for me," he said, his breath coming faster as Erin obeyed. She reached down, grabbing the inside of her thighs and pulling them apart, baring her pussy to his gaze.

His cock throbbed as he took her in. Her delicate outer lips were a deep pink and plump with the force of her desire. Just above, her clit stood firm and erect, and between her folds, her entrance glistened, already dripping. She was hot and ready for him, and he was past ready to have another taste of his girl.

"Wider." He grunted his approval as she moved her hands behind her knees, tugging them up and out, baring every inch of her sex from clit to ass, offering herself to him completely, without hesitation or fear.

It was enough to snap the last of his

control.

With a groan, he lowered his face between her legs, forcing himself to start slowly, to trace the swollen folds and tease her into an even greater state of arousal. He ran his tongue up one side of her entrance and down the other, intensifying his pressure until she moaned and arched closer to his mouth. Only then did he drive slowly inside her, once, twice, her addictive flavor coating his stiff tongue, making his hands shake as he brought them to her hips. His fingers dug into the full flesh there as he began to fuck her with his mouth. In and out, in and out, he penetrated her with his swift strokes, coaxing more cream from her body.

"Yes! So good." Erin's hands dropped to his head, her fingernails tunneling through his short hair and digging into his scalp.

Blake moaned, humming against her swollen flesh, making her cry out as he moved his thumb to her nub. He circled her clit with a slow, insistent pressure even as the thrusts of his tongue grew faster, deeper. Erin's pussy tightened around where he worked inside her and her thighs began to tremble. A glance up the landscape of her body showed her nipples were drawn into tight points and her head thrown back in prelude to ecstasy.

She was close, so close, but he wasn't finished with her just yet.

Without missing a beat, Blake moved his mouth from her entrance to her clit, swirling his tongue around and around the erect bud. Two fingers took up the rhythm inside her pussy, while his thumb found the puckered ring of her ass. She was already slick from her own juices, so there was little resistance as he penetrated her, easing his thumb inside the tight hole.

"Yes!" Erin gasped and spread her thighs even wider, giving him unimpeded access to every inch of the paradise between her legs.

She clearly didn't have a problem with having him fill her anywhere and everywhere. It made him ache to have his cock in her ass.

Anal wasn't his favorite way to fuck—not by a long shot—but it was the only way he hadn't had Erin and he wanted to fuck her everywhere. He wanted to mark her mouth and her pussy and her ass, fill her up with him until she couldn't remember any cock giving her pleasure except his.

The thought made him impossibly harder. He wanted to explore every inch of her body and make it clear she belonged to him, would *always* belong to him.

"Oh please, oh please." Erin panted above him, eager sounds issuing from the back of her throat. "Can I come? Blake, can I—"

"Come for me, beautiful. Come on my mouth," he mumbled against her aroused flesh. He sucked her clit, drawing hard on the nub until Erin came with a wild cry.

She bucked beneath him, heels digging into the mattress, pelvis lifting into the air. Blake moved his hands back to her hips, holding her still as he gently lapped away the slickness rushing down her thighs. Only when her breath began to slow and some of the tension left her muscles did he increase the pressure of his strokes once more, playing through her folds with his tongue, teasing her clit with the barest pressure.

"I don't know if I can go again," she whispered, hands shaking as her fingers combed through his hair. "It was so amazing, Blake. So intense. I'm not all the way back in my body yet."

"You will be," he promised, continuing his tender torment, licking and probing until Erin's hands fisted in the sheets and her soft whimpers of arousal filled the air. Finally, her needy sounds and the smell of the fresh heat pooling between her legs was too much to resist. He needed to be inside her, needed to fuck her with all the desire coursing through his veins like a runaway train.

Blake surged over Erin's trembling body, positioning himself and shoving his engorged, aching cock into where she was so hot, so wet.

"Fuck, Erin." He groaned into her mouth, meeting her eager lips with his own, slipping his tongue between her teeth and letting her taste her own salty heat.

She wrapped her legs around his hips and squeezed, urging him even deeper inside her welcoming sheath. "Yes! You feel so good, Blake."

The head of his cock bumped against the end of her and his balls fit snugly in the crack of her ass, but still Erin flexed her muscles and tilted her hips as if she couldn't get him deep enough. Blake knew how she felt. He wanted to get closer, deeper. He wanted to share her skin, to fuse their separate bodies into one mass of pulsing, aroused flesh.

With a growl, Blake pulled back and slammed home, again and again, burying himself to the hilt in Erin. Slow, savage thrusts all too quickly became swift and desperate as his control slipped, burned away by the heat they generated together. He rode her hard, shoving in and out of her slick sheath, setting a brutal rhythm Erin matched with eager lifts of her hips.

"Yes, Blake. Yes!" She came without warning this time, her pussy clamping down on where he moved inside her, triggering his own release so quickly he barely had time to realize he wasn't wearing a condom.

CHAPTER ELEVEN

Blake

Blake cursed as he pulled out of her tight heat, his cock pulsing against her belly, spilling thick, sticky cum across her stomach.

He groaned as his release rocketed through him, sending waves of satisfaction flowing out to every inch of his body, the pleasure at odds with the voice inside his head that shouted that he was a fucking idiot for forgetting protection.

He collapsed on top of Erin a few seconds later, breath still coming faster as he pressed a soft kiss to her lips. "I'm so sorry about that."

"Don't worry," she panted. "I like feeling you come on me." She kissed him again, her arms wrapping around him, fingertips tracing patterns on his sweat-dampened back.

He sighed. "No, I meant for forgetting a condom."

"Oh," she said, blinking as comprehension dawned. "Well, I'm on the pill and clean. So you don't have to worry about my end of things."

"I'm clean, too. I was tested a couple of months ago and I *never* forget to wear a rubber," he said, not realizing how true the words were until they were out of his mouth.

He had truly *never* forgotten to use protection. Not a single time in his life. No wonder he'd come so fast. He wasn't used to the bliss of being inside a woman without a latex barrier, especially this woman.

Erin. God. Fucking her was even better than it had been when they were kids. So fucking hot he wanted her again, ten seconds after they'd finished.

"This was the first time this has happened," he confessed. "Ever. I don't know what I was thinking. I shouldn't have lost control."

"Some Dom you are," she said, a teasing gleam in her eye. "I think *you* should be punished this time."

He smiled. "I think you're right. How about I serve you waffles on my hands and knees?" He bent his head, pressing kisses along her bare shoulder. It was impossible to keep from kissing her when she was this close.

"I was thinking you could grab me a towel from the bathroom," she said with a giggle. "But the hands and knees stuff sounds good, too."

"Yes, ma'am. Your wish is my command." Blake rolled out of bed and headed into the bathroom, taking a second to wash his hands and run warm water on a washcloth before returning to Erin with the cloth and a towel. "I have returned, Mistress."

Erin laughed as she wrinkled her nose. "Do you switch? I mean, I can't imagine it, but I have to ask."

"No, never," he said with a smile. "Do you?"

"No. Being submissive feels right to me," she said, adding in a lightly offended tone, "no matter what you may think."

Blake remembered his words from the night before and felt guilty. "Maybe I was too quick to judge. We haven't spent enough time in bed for me to know anything for sure."

"A Dom admitting he might have been wrong?" Her eyes grew comically large. "Is the world coming to an end?"

"I don't know what kind of 'Doms' you've been dealing with, but I admit I'm wrong all the time. I'm only human," he said, then added with a grin, "Though an exceptionally hot human."

"Yes, you are," Erin purred, stretching luxuriously. "That was…amazing. I haven't felt this perfect in a long, long time."

"Me either." He sat down on the bed, trying not to think too much about how hot the sex had been, or the fact that no one but Erin had ever left him with a feeling of such bone-deep satisfaction. "Scoot over, beautiful. Let me clean you up."

"Thanks." She moved closer, eyes sliding shut as he ran the warm rag over her skin. "That feels good." She paused, a grin spreading across her face. "Your cum still smells the same. Like green apple slices, with salt on them."

"You never told me that," he said as he wiped away the last of the stickiness and began to dry her with the towel.

Her eyes blinked open as she shrugged. "Yeah, well. I was shy."

"Right," he said with a snort of disbelief.

"I was!" She laughed, that same musical

laugh that had haunted his dreams for years. "Besides, I thought all cum smelled like that. You were my first encounter of the cum-y kind."

His smile faded. "I remember."

Erin's stomach rose and fell and a strained silence stretched between them. He didn't know what she was thinking about, but he was thinking about their first time together, her first time with anyone, and how desperately he'd wanted to make it perfect for the girl he loved.

Blake knelt between Erin's spread legs, hands trembling as he slid the condom onto his aching length, his pulse roaring in his ears.

"Now, Blake. Please." Erin reached her arms out to him, the hunger in her voice matching his own.

He stretched over her, meeting her lips for a kiss as he positioned himself at her entrance—just touching, but not pushing inside. He'd already brought her over with his tongue and she was soaked, but her pussy was so tight.

He had to go slow to fit two fingers into her heat;

he couldn't imagine a scenario where his cock inside of her wasn't going to cause her pain.

Fear of hurting her gave him the strength to hold still, no matter how desperately he wanted to thrust his hips forward.

"Are you sure?" he asked again, nudging her gently with the head of his throbbing erection, testing her entrance, not surprised when he met resistance.

"I'm sure." She cupped his face in her hands, gazing up at him with love in her eyes. "I know it's going to hurt a little, but I want you so much I don't care. I need to feel you inside me." She wrapped her legs around his waist and lifted her hips. "Now, Blake. Please."

Jaw clenched as he fought for control, Blake began to rock against her, keeping his thrusts shallow, giving her body time to adjust. Once the first few inches of his cock were inside her pussy, it became almost impossible to go slow.

Her slick heat gripped him like a fist. She was so wet, so tight, and felt so damned good he could have come in ten seconds. But he forced himself to maintain his slow, gentle rhythm, gliding in and out until every inch of his cock was buried inside of her.

"Okay?" he asked, brushing her hair from her face.

"Perfect," she breathed.

Their eyes met and held and a hundred promises passed between them.

It was perfect. So perfect Blake silently swore that this was going to be his last first time. This was what making love was supposed to feel like, and he didn't want to make love to anyone else, ever again.

He just wanted Erin. For keeps.

Throat tight, Blake stood, crossing the room to throw the towel and rag in the dirty-clothes basket. The decorator really had thought of everything. The getaway was so comfortable, a part of him wished he could stay forever.

Forget Miami and his and Rafe's tattooing empire. He could live here in the woods with Erin, happy as a pig in shit.

Too bad that scenario was about as impossible as they came.

Is it? Look at her. She still cares about you.

This weekend might have a happier ending than you could have imagined before you and Erin hooked up again.

Blake pushed the thought away. He couldn't let himself start thinking forever thoughts about him and Erin. That path led to nothing but heartache. He'd just have to enjoy this weekend for what it was—forty-eight hours of fun and hot sex, nothing more.

"You want me to go down and start the waffle batter?" Erin asked as he turned back to the bed, her head emerging from her nightshirt.

She'd decided to get dressed. Probably a good thing, or their chances of getting out of this bedroom today weren't going to be good. Still, he couldn't help wishing she were still naked. He wanted to soak up the sight of her, memorize the location of every freckle before they went their separate ways.

"I knew a guy once who called cum baby batter," she continued with a nervous laugh. "So gross."

"I don't want to hear about guys you've known," he said, the idea of anyone else with Erin making him unreasonably cranky.

"He wasn't a lover." She blushed as she threw him his boxer briefs and pajama pants, then turned, presumably hunting for her underwear. Blake saw her panties lying on the floor, but decided to let her look for a while, enjoying the glimpses of her pussy as she bent over to look under the bed.

"He was a guy I worked with at this restaurant in Santa Monica," she continued, locating her panties and pulling them on. "He had ten kids. *Ten.* That's too much of a good thing if you ask me."

"How many kids is enough of a good thing?" Blake asked, ignoring the part of him that said those kinds of questions were the dangerous breed of stupid.

He and Erin were never even going to date again, let alone shack up and start making babies together. How many kids she did or didn't want was none of his business.

"I don't know. That's a hard question," she said softly, a wistful look on her face that reminded him she wasn't the girl he'd known eight years ago. That girl wouldn't get upset talking about babies. Even at sixteen, Erin had talked about wanting a big family and kids she would lavish with all the love she and Blake had missed out on.

"I always thought I wanted three," she continued. "But now I think two might be enough.

"What changed your mind?"

"I've done some babysitting for girlfriends. Newborns are a *lot* of work. Especially if you don't have any help." She shrugged before crossing her arms at her chest. "My husband didn't like to touch anything human under eighteen years of age. He wasn't much help on the nights I was on babysitting duty."

Blake grunted. "Afraid he would break them?"

She shook her head. "No, he called them blobs. Said they weren't people until they could do something other than sleep, mess themselves, and cry."

"He sounds like a winner," Blake said, unable to keep the anger from his voice.

What the hell had Erin been doing with a man like that? Hadn't she learned enough self-respect to know she deserved better? She'd always despised Phil's wife for being a doormat to her abusive husband, yet it looked like she'd ended up in a very similar situation.

"Scott is a piece of shit, but I didn't know that when we got married," she said as if she'd read his thoughts. He shouldn't be surprised. They'd always been eerily connected when they were younger, finishing each other's sentences so often their friends would make fun of them for it.

"At first things were good, or at least okay," she said. "But then…situations developed and things changed."

His eyes narrowed. "What kind of situations?"

"Just unexpected things." Erin shuddered,

the memories of her marriage bad enough to cause a physical response. "But I don't really want to talk about the stupid decisions I've made. Let's go make breakfast and you can catch me up on the dumb things you've done in the past eight years. Make me feel better about myself."

"Assuming I've done dumb things." Blake forced a smile, trying to lighten the mood, but a part of him wanted to keep pushing at Erin, to find out what she was hiding.

She was definitely hiding something, there was no doubt in his mind.

Of course, if he found out her ex had hit her or manipulated her with the threat of violence the way their foster father had his wife, Blake wouldn't be able to rest until he did something about it. And unfortunately for him, he was no longer a minor who could get away with beating the shit out of any guy who hurt his girl.

His girl.

A part of him wanted nothing more than to

be able to say those words and have them be true. He wanted Erin to be his again. For now, and for as long as he could have her. Of all the things he'd worried about when he'd planned this weekend, begging her to give them another chance was the very last thing he'd anticipated. But with every moment they spent together it was becoming more apparent that their past wasn't going to stay in the past.

"I'm betting you've done a stupid thing or two." Erin took his hand and pulled him through the bathroom into the bedroom where he'd passed a restless night, knowing he was so close to her. "There's no way you went straight from law-abiding citizen to kidnapper without a few stops in between."

"Considering you're my kidnap victim," Blake said, his stomach cramping, "I'm not sure you should be making jokes about that."

Erin paused at the top of the stairs and turned back to him, looking up at him with her fathomless eyes. "I know you would never hurt me, Blake. Not *really* hurt me."

"Even when I alter your tattoo tomorrow?" The guilt that washed over him at the idea of doing anything to Erin against her will was so strong it sickened him.

The longer he spent with her—talking to her, making love to her, laughing with her— the smaller the chance he was actually going to go through with what he'd planned.

She dropped his hand and crossed her arms, the defensive gesture making her look smaller. "Well, if that happens, I certainly won't respect you as much as I do now, or trust you. But I'll be okay. You'd have to take a lot more than a tattoo away from me to break me."

Before he could think of what to say to that—or how to convince Erin the last thing he wanted to do was break her—she'd turned and started down the stairs. A moment later, she was in the kitchen, voice raised as she asked him how strong he wanted his coffee.

But he couldn't seem to concentrate on her words, not when his head was spinning.

Losing Erin's respect and trust meant a lot more now than it would have before they started down the road to power exchange. His gut reaction to the thought was another nauseating twist of his stomach.

He didn't want to lose her trust. Hell, he didn't want to lose *her*, period.

Even remembering the way she'd betrayed him didn't give him a leg to stand on anymore. If he abused the faith she'd so readily placed in him—both in the bedroom and out—he was going to be a more wretched person than she'd ever been.

And she'd only been sixteen years old, not much more than a kid, and their lives hadn't been easy back then. He was a successful man with a promising career, friends, money, security—in short, everything he and Erin had ever dreamed of. If he forced his will upon a woman who was obviously not in the best place in her life from that place of safety, Erin would be right to never trust him again.

He would be as much of a monster as her

former husband.

With those cheery thoughts swirling through his mind, Blake headed down the stairs, no longer certain how this weekend was going to end, just wishing it didn't have to end at all.

CHAPTER TWELVE

Erin

Erin didn't know why she was surprised that Blake could Cook with a capital *C*, but she was.

Even after she'd consumed her half of a tomato, basil, and goat cheese frittata and polished off two gingerbread waffles, made from batter she'd watched Blake whip up from scratch, she couldn't quite wrap her head around it. After all, just because the only other Dom she'd had breakfast with couldn't fry an egg to save his life, it didn't mean all Dominant men were the same.

Blake had already demonstrated an abundance of differences between himself and her soon-to-be ex. Not the least of which was an insatiable desire for her after-baby body. He didn't seem to notice that her breasts sagged a little and had stretch marks on the sides, or that the skin on her stomach wasn't as tight as it used to be. She'd hit the gym every day in hopes of resuming her career and knew she looked good enough to model, but there were things a lover saw that Photoshop took care of before photographs were published.

But Blake didn't seem to notice the marks childbirth had left behind.

Or if he did, he obviously didn't find them repulsive.

"You want the last one?" he asked, pausing

with his fork halfway to the last waffle on the plate between them.

"No, thank you." She sat back in her chair with a contented sigh. "I'm stuffed. I shouldn't have finished that second one, but I'm a sucker for real maple syrup. Soooo good."

"Yeah, not like that fake butter-flavored crap we used to eat in high school." He smiled. "Remember when we fixed the little kids pancakes for dinner?"

Erin nodded, noticing Blake didn't refer to the other kids by name, either. No matter how much they'd both tried to help the other minors unlucky enough to end up in Phil's house, they had kept their emotional distance. It was the only way to stay sane when you were underage and helpless to change anyone's life, including your own.

"They thought it was so cool we were having breakfast for dinner," she said. "Like it was a special occasion."

"When really we just didn't have anything

else to feed them."

"Yeah. Good times." Erin crossed her legs in her chair and reached for her coffee. "But I'm more interested in hearing some new dirt. I thought you were going to give me the goods on the lifestyles of the rich and famous."

"I was on a reality show on an arts station." He shrugged as if he really thought it was no big deal that he'd been on national television every week.

Of course, knowing Blake, he probably *didn't* think it was a big deal. He'd never wanted to be a star. Not like she had when she was younger and certain she was going to set the modeling world on fire.

Now she'd settle for making a decent living for her and Abby.

Abby. Her chest tightened miserably every time she thought her sweet baby's name. It was getting harder to hold the pain at a distance. She sensed it had something to do with Blake and the way he was slowly, but surely, worming his way back into her heart, but she was trying not to think about that too much. If suffering through her miserable marriage had taught her one thing, it was that thinking too far ahead was a good way to make the load you carried too heavy to handle.

"I'd hardly call that famous," Blake continued, cutting his waffle into smaller squares. "Probably more people know your name than mine."

She lifted a dubious brow. "Highly doubtful."

"From what I hear, your picture was on half the billboards in L.A."

"That was almost two years ago." She shook her head, remembering how bizarre it had been to see herself blown up ten feet tall. "In Los Angeles time that's eons ago. I'm old news."

"You're still the featured model on the Damned Naughty Web site."

She shrugged as she swirled her last drink

of coffee in a circle at the bottom of her cup. "I'm sure that's just because they've been too lazy to change the template. My body is part of the banner."

"Yeah, I've seen it," he said, his voice dropping half a register. "That red corset thing is…very nice."

Erin laughed. "Thank you, but stop trying to change the subject. I want to hear about you."

"Me." He sighed as he scooted his chair back and began to gather up the breakfast dishes. He hadn't served her on his hands and knees like he'd promised, but he had cooked, set the table, and motioned for her to stay seated as he continued cleaning up.

A Dominant man who didn't mind serving as well as being served. She'd never dreamed such a person existed, and knew she'd be falling for Blake even if this were the first time they'd ever met.

"Let's see," he said as he set the dirty plates in the sink. "After high school, I did the part-time tattoo artist, part-time bouncer thing. I built up a nice portfolio in the first six months and started planning my move to Reno."

"Just like you said you would." She smiled, but it felt sad on her face. "Good for you."

"But then I got an offer to move to Vegas and work as a bouncer for some new club," he said. "They were looking for a certain type and I fit the bill."

She lifted a brow as she watched the powerful man her high school love had become stride back toward the table. "The tall, sexy, scary type?"

"Something like that." His lips quirked as he poured himself another cup of coffee and then refilled her cup before easing back into his chair. "So you think I'm sexy?"

"No, I've been faking all those orgasms," she said with a wink.

His lip quirk became a smile. "You're an excellent actress."

"I'm thinking about trying my hand at an acting career if the modeling thing doesn't work out." She grinned at him over the rim of her cup.

"Really?" he asked. "I bet you'd be great."

"No, not really." She rolled her eyes. "I'd have no idea what I was doing. I'd be terrible, and even if I weren't, modeling is bad enough. I'd have a nervous breakdown if there were paparazzi stalking my every move."

He laughed. "So the famous thing isn't as great as you thought it would be, huh? Hate to say I told you so, but…"

Erin's eyes narrowed in Blake's direction. "No, you don't. You love it. You always did. Must have been the Dom in you, dying to come out and impose his will on people in need of his guidance."

"I don't know about that." He glanced down at his coffee. "I just thought you'd be happier doing something more low-key. You always hated it when people paid too much attention to you at school. I couldn't imagine the attention of strangers would be any better."

She sighed, floored by how well he'd known her, even better than she'd known herself back then. "You were right," she said softly. "It was weird getting that much attention, especially lingerie-model kind of attention. But by the time I got the Damned Naughty gig, I was tired of working twelve-hour waitressing shifts to pay my rent. The money made up for the weirdness."

He nodded. "Money does help. I was against the reality show idea at the beginning, but my partner, Rafe, was right to push me into it. It was amazing free publicity. Quadrupled our business in the first year."

They talked for another hour and drank their way through a third pot of coffee, the conversation flowing more smoothly than any in Erin's recent memory.

How long had it been since she'd been able to sit and have a relaxing conversation with a good friend? It seemed like forever. And she'd never felt so at home and relaxed with any man but Blake.

Scott had been the type of man who liked to keep his Dom hat on twenty-four seven. At first, twenty-one-year-old Erin—who was new to the scene and hooked on the high of subbing for the first time—had thought that was a wonderful thing. But after six months, she'd started to crave some downtime. Time when they could just be comfortable together. She'd started to wish for a Dominant and submissive relationship where the different roles underscored their relationship like music, not smothered it like a wool blanket.

It wouldn't be like that with Blake. She could just feel it.

Sitting across from him at the breakfast table already felt achingly familiar. They'd never had a chance to live together, just the two of them, but this was how she'd always dreamed it would be. Hell, it was better than she'd dreamed it would be. In her younger fantasies, she hadn't known how much she craved the thrill of submitting to a Dominant man or guessed that her first love would grow up to be her dream guy.

Of course, she should have known. Blake had always been a knight in shining armor, the kind of brave, confident, caring man who seemed extinct in modern times. Even in the BDSM club scene it was rare to find a man in possession of himself the way Blake was. A lot of crazies who lacked the personality or finesse to win a woman in the "real world" assumed they could come into a club and find a docile submissive to put up with all their crap.

A true Dom was a hard thing to find.

"So how did you get into the scene anyway?" Erin asked, not realizing she'd propped her toes on the edge of Blake's chair until he took a foot in hand and began to run his thumbs along her instep. "Breakfast and a foot rub? I must have been a very good girl."

He laughed beneath his breath. "You were."

"I tried to use the shower nozzle last night," Erin said, the confession spilling from her lips before she could think better of it.

The compulsion to be honest with Blake was just too strong. No matter what her rational mind had to say, her inner sub wanted to turn over control to this man, to trust him with every thought, every secret.

"I wasn't planning on obeying that last order," she continued. "I just...I wanted you to know."

He didn't pause in his massaging of her feet, but Erin saw the muscle in his jaw tense. "So what changed your mind?"

"My body."

He raised an eyebrow, silently urging her to continue.

"I couldn't come," she whispered. "Not without your permission."

"You *couldn't?*" he asked, sounding more curious than angry.

"I physically couldn't. And I tried, believe me." She bit her lip as she set her empty coffee cup back on the table. "But a part of me wanted to please you too much."

Blake stared at her for a few minutes, his dark eyes unreadable. When he finally spoke, his silky Dom voice was back in full effect. "That's one of the hottest things I've ever heard."

"Yeah?" she asked, a part of her hoping he'd prove it by tackling her to the floor of the kitchen and showing her just how hot he was.

But he only smiled and turned his attention back to her feet. "Yeah."

"Well...good," Erin said, ignoring the heat pooling in her belly. She couldn't be ready for more already. It had only been a couple of hours since she'd come so hard she was sure she'd done herself damage. "So are you going to tell me how you got into the scene?"

"My first girlfriend after I moved to Vegas was interested in checking out this dungeon they had going at the edge of town," he said. "She had fantasies about getting chained to a wall by a man wearing black leather."

She grinned. "Sounds fun."

Blake laughed. "She thought so, too, until she was all strapped in. Then she couldn't get out of her restraints or that club fast enough. Turns out the BDSM scene wasn't for her. But I liked it just fine."

Erin squirmed slightly in her chair, finding it damned difficult to consider Blake's foot rub relaxing instead of arousing. "Yeah, some people just want to have the fantasy. But not me. When I first discovered the BDSM clubs in L.A., I wanted to live there. All the time."

"I can imagine."

"Can you?" she asked, voice hitching as Blake's thumb dug into her arch.

"You're excited right now. Aren't you?" He pinned her with a look she felt sizzle across her skin. "After we spent half the night and all morning playing, you want more."

Erin nodded slowly. Within seconds, her breath grew faster and her pussy wet simply from watching the heat flare in Blake's eyes.

"You can't get enough," he said, continuing when Erin shook her head again. "So why don't you take that shirt off. I have something I want you to put on while we finish talking."

Erin couldn't obey fast enough.

CHAPTER THIRTEEN

Erin

Erin's hands were trembling as she stripped her nightshirt off and threw it to the ground, amazed that the moment had gone from comfortable to erotic so quickly.

It was incredibly arousing.

Almost as arousing as the sight of what Blake had fished from the kitchen drawer.

"I didn't bring my nipple clamps, but I

think these will work just fine." Blake knelt in front of her, setting the clothespins on the table before placing his hands lightly on her hips. "Would you like me to put those on your nipples?"

"Yes." Her breasts were already aching, her nipples drawing into tight points despite the warmth of the room. "Very much."

"I thought you might." Blake held her eyes as he lowered his mouth, capturing one aching tip between his lips. He suckled her gently at first, teasing her with the tip of his tongue, swirling around and around the taut bud until Erin's eyes slid closed on a moan.

"Open your eyes, watch me," he said, his words sending a jolt of arousal searing along her nerves, and more heat pooling between her thighs. "And don't move until I give you permission."

Erin met Blake's eyes again as he plucked one of the clothespins from the table and attached it to her nipple. The pinching sensation only intensified her desire, the pain and pleasure fusing together to create an arousing sensation more powerful than either one alone.

Blake waited until she regained a measure of control over her rapid breathing before transferring his attention to her other breast, licking, sucking and biting, driving her mad with the need to move. It was hellish work not to squirm in her seat, not to thread her fingers through Blake's hair and hold on for dear life.

But she wanted his approval and the reward for her obedience—which she had no doubt he would deliver—far more than the small relief movement would afford.

"Good, so good." Blake breathed the words against her breast, then flicked his tongue out across her nipple one last time, making her gasp. He attached the second clothespin, his own breath coming faster.

"So, what have you been doing for the past two years?" he asked, still on his knees in front of her. "Why did you quit modeling?"

"D-do we really have to talk?" she asked, her voice thin and strained.

"I think we should give the clamps some time, don't you?" His calm tone and the relaxed way he reclaimed his chair would have been enough to make her scream if his excitement weren't abundantly obvious. The front of his pajama pants was tented where his erection strained the fabric.

Erin could see the outline of the bulbous head of his cock through the thin material and it was enough to make her mouth water. She wanted his cock back in her mouth. She wanted to suck him until he cried out in that way that made her positive no one had ever given him the kind of pleasure she had.

She wanted to swallow down every last drop of his cum and then keep sucking him until he was hard again, until he pulled his thick length from her mouth and shoved it between her legs. There wouldn't be any foreplay aside from the nipple clamps, but she knew she'd be wet. Though, hopefully, not too wet. She loved the hint of pain as he forced himself inside her during those first few moments. The resistance of her body, the sting as he demanded entrance, took her halfway to orgasm in one earth-shattering thrust.

"What are you thinking about?" he asked, his voice thick with lust.

"How much I want to suck your cock." Erin met his eyes but didn't move an inch from her present position, determined to show him she could be good. "I was thinking about how hot it felt to have your hand fisted in my hair, to feel you fucking my mouth."

"What about your ass?" he asked. "Because I want your ass to belong to me, too."

"We'd need lube," she said, her pussy getting wetter despite the fact that anal had been her least favorite activity with her ex. Somehow, she knew that would be as different with Blake as everything else. "But I want you to fuck me any way you want."

His expression grew stormy with desire and

Erin's pinched nipples tingled and stung. "Would that turn you on?"

"Yes." The word emerged as a moan as she imagined Blake forcing her to her hands and knees and taking her in the ass. She could practically feel his large hand landing stinging slaps to her bottom as his cock stroked deep inside her. "And I'd...I'd like you to spank me while you fucked me."

"Spank you, and call you my dirty girl?" he asked, leaning forward with his elbows on his knees until his lips were only inches away from her mouth.

"Yes. Please, yes." Erin swept her tongue across her lips, her entire body screaming with the need to be touched, with the need to throw her arms around Blake and never let him go.

"Why do you like to hear those words from a man, Erin?" he asked, his eyes drifting to her lips.

"I don't like to hear them from a man. I'd like to hear them from you."

"You didn't like your husband to—"

"No, I didn't," she said, the sound of the word "husband" on Blake's lips making her ill. She couldn't wait for the day when Scott would no longer hold that title. "He would say them, but I never got off on it. But I would with you."

"Why?" He moved one hand to her face, tracing a soft finger along her jaw. "Why is it different with me?"

"I don't know...I guess..." For the third time in less than a day, tears threatened at the backs of her eyes.

There was something about being with Blake that turned her inside out, that pushed her to wander the edges of her own emotional landscape. It was what she'd always heard a good Dom would do, but she'd never been there, never been forced to look into another person's eyes and know they were seeing straight through to the core of her.

But here she was and there was the answer to his question, suddenly floating in the air in front of her. "I'd like it because I'd know you didn't really think I was dirty. That, to you, it would be a term of endearment."

"It would." He nodded. "What else?"

"I know you wouldn't say it to just anyone," she said, tongue slipping out to dampen her lips. "So it would make me feel special."

"And why wouldn't I say it to just anyone?" he asked, his lips moving closer to hers, so close she was certain he would kiss her, but he stopped when there were still a few inches between them. "Why would I only say it to you?"

"Because…" Erin sucked in a deep breath, fighting tears, refusing to let the liquid pooling in her eyes spill down her cheeks no matter how scary and emotional this moment had become. "Because you care about me?"

"I do," Blake whispered. "So much, Erin. So fucking much."

Erin started crying then, she couldn't seem to help herself. She was sobbing when Blake pressed a kiss to her lips and pulled her into his arms, tears rolling down the cheek she pressed against his chest as he carried her across the room.

CHAPTER FOURTEEN

Blake

Blake laid Erin down on the soft carpet by the fire and hovered above her, dropping kisses across her forehead as she cried, for the first time in his life not bothered by a woman's tears.

She wasn't crying because she was sad. She was crying because sometimes it hurt to learn that someone cared about you. When you'd convinced yourself there was no goodness or softness left in the world, at least not for you, the unexpectedness of a tender emotion could be overwhelming.

He knew that's how she felt because he felt the same way.

"I still love you, Erin." He whispered his confession against her lips, feeling close to tears himself as she brought trembling fingers to his face, her touch communicating more emotion than he'd thought possible.

"I love you, too, Blake. I'm so sorry I ever left, I'm sorry—"

"It doesn't matter." He silenced her with a kiss, a real kiss this time, slipping his tongue into her mouth, tasting coffee and maple syrup and Erin. He kissed her until both of them were breathless before he pulled back to look her in the eyes. "I don't care about the past. I only care about the future."

"Can we have a future?" she asked, fear creeping back into her voice. "There's so much we don't know about each other, so much—"

"We can have whatever we decide to have." He captured her chin between his fingers and thumb, willing her to see that they had to seize this second chance, no matter how crazy it might seem. "More importantly, we can have whatever *I* say we can have."

"Because you're the big bad Dom?" she asked with a sad, crooked smile.

"Because I'm *your* big bad Dom," he said, knowing his eyes were shining, but not giving a damn. "And you're my girl. I love you so much, Erin. I swear to you I will never treat you badly or abuse your trust."

"I know you wouldn't, Blake. But it's been eight years." She sucked in a breath and shifted her gaze to stare at a place above his head. "And there are things you don't know about me, things that might change your mind."

"We can talk about those things when you're ready," Blake said, sensing it wasn't the time to push Erin to reveal her secrets. "But I can tell you right now I don't care about what's happened in the past eight years. No matter what you've done, if you were mine, I'd still feel like the luckiest man in the world."

"You would?" Her bottom lip trembled.

"I would, but you've got to stop crying." He laughed, a strained sound that grew easier when Erin laughed with him. "Or I'm going to start."

"You are not," she said, a hesitant smile spreading across her face.

He could sense how much she wanted to believe that this was a new beginning for them. But he could also feel the doubt that lingered in her mind.

This wasn't the kind of thing that was going to be resolved in a few minutes and pushing Erin right now would do no good. It was time to get them back on more comfortable ground. Even as kids, they hadn't been big into talking feelings, no matter how strong they'd been. They had always preferred to let actions speak louder than words.

With one deft movement, he gripped the waistband of her panties and pulled them off.

"What if I said I was going to fuck my pussy? Would you believe that?" As he spoke, he trailed one hand up the inside of her thigh, teasing at the crease where leg became something more intimate. He could feel the heat coming from her core before he touched her and it was enough to make him even harder.

"Yes, I would," she said, sucking in a breath as he brushed one finger up the length of her, catching moisture from her pussy and moving it to her clit.

"Now, the only question is: How am I going to fuck you?" As he spoke, he began to circle her nub, making Erin squirm beneath him and a sigh burst from between her parted lips. "Am I going to take you like this, on top? Or am I going to flip you over and lift your hips and take you from behind?"

"Yes and yes," she said, twining her arms

around his neck as she spread her thighs even farther, a clear invitation to do with her as he would.

"Or should I pull you on top of me? Let you ride my cock while I suck my tits?" He accentuated the last word by flicking the clothespins still attached to her nipples, making Erin groan. "Are you ready for these to come off?"

"I don't care. I just want you to fuck me," she said, the strength of her desire clear in her eyes. "Now."

"Are you giving orders?"

"No, but I'm ready to take them." She released her hold on his neck, stretching her arms out to her sides, awaiting his command. "Tell me what you want, Blake. Tell me how to please you."

His chest tightened and his aching sac threatened to burst as he looked down at Erin, suddenly longing to dispense with the Dom-sub play and let this time be different.

He didn't just want to fuck. He wanted to

make love. He wanted to show Erin with every stroke of his cock how much he loved her. He wanted to kiss her softly as he slid between her thighs, whisper all the things he'd held inside as he thrust in and out of her tight heat.

"If you don't tell me how to please you, I might have to start pleasing myself," Erin teased, a naughty grin on her face as she moved one hand to her stomach and then slid her fingers lower.

"If you touch my pussy, you'll be punished. And it won't be that spanking I know you're after." Blake grabbed her wrist and pulled it away from her body. "Turn over. Forearms on the ground, hips in the air. Show me my pussy."

"Yes, sir." Erin smiled as she said the words, but he read the excitement—and relief—in her eyes.

She wasn't ready to make love, not yet. They were both dealing with some unexpected and heavy emotions. He wanted to deal with them by delving right into the middle of things. She would rather distract herself. Erin needed to be fucked, controlled, taken in order to feel safe from the feelings that were scaring her. Blake realized that and was prepared to give her exactly what she needed. There would be time for making love later.

He and Erin were too perfect for each other to let a second chance slip through their fingers. They were meant to be together, a matching set, just like their tattoos.

"I think we'll have to leave this exactly as is," he said, leaning over and pressing a kiss to the angel tat on her shoulder. "It's not bothering me to have the same ink anymore."

"It's not?" she asked, her voice breathy with excitement as he ran his hands down her thighs to her knees and tugged them farther apart.

"No, I like to see my mark on you. Now tilt your hips." Blake sat back on his heels, grunting in satisfaction as Erin arched her back and shifted her pelvis, giving him a clear view of his pussy.

Her flesh was dark rose, and her lips plumped to a point that they looked bruised. At the center of her sex, her entrance leaked clear fluid down her thighs. She was as aroused as he'd ever seen her. Either the nipple clamps or the love talk had done the job of at least a half hour of foreplay.

Call him a romantic, but he hoped it was emotion that had made his pussy so wet. Still, he made a mental note to invest in a set of high-end clamps as soon as possible. If clothespins made his girl this crazy, he'd like to see what a nice set of metal screw clamps would do.

He could imagine himself and Erin in his new condo in Miami, cooking dinner together, Erin with her clamps on as they set the table and ate. They'd linger over a glass of wine and then he'd have her dripping pussy for dessert, right there by the windows that looked out over the ocean.

Just imagining the scene made his chest ache.

He wanted that. He wanted it as much as he'd ever wanted anything.

"Blake, please." Erin moaned and arched her back even farther, making it clear how desperately she wanted him to touch her, fuck her.

Any other time he would have made her wait, teased her into a state of even greater arousal. But not now, not when her need was so obvious and his cock felt like it was going to explode if he didn't get inside her ten minutes ago.

Seconds later, Blake was out of his pants and kneeling behind her, fingers digging into her hips as the head of his cock butted against her entrance. He didn't use his hands to position himself or spread the lips of her pussy to ease his way. He simply thrust forward as he tugged her hips back, shoving his engorged length inside her. Erin's sigh of pleasure made it clear she loved the hint of resistance as much as he did.

Slowly, drawing out the bliss of that first thrust into where she was so tight, so wet, Blake pushed forward until he was buried to the hilt, his balls pressed tightly against her clit. "Jesus, Erin. My pussy is so wet."

Erin wiggled her hips, taking him in even deeper. "You make me that way, I can't help it," she said, a shudder of desire working through her body as her pussy tightened around where he lay buried inside her. "Fuck me now, Blake. Please fuck me."

Blake grunted, delivering a sharp smack on the cheek of her ass, his cock swelling inside her as she cried out in excitement. "Do you want me to spank you while I fuck you?"

"Yes," she said, another cry escaping her lips as he swatted her other cheek. "Yes, sir. Please. Please!"

Blake brought his hands back to her hips, digging his fingers into the full flesh with enough force to make her moan as pain and pleasure fused together. The tension in the muscles trembling beneath his hands made it clear Erin wouldn't last much longer. A few more cracks of his hand and she was going to come before he had a chance to thrust inside her a second time.

Normally he'd be glad to feel her come at least once before he did himself, but not now. Not even thinking of dead puppies or his grandmother's underpants was going to help him maintain control if Erin's pussy started pulsing around his aching cock. He was too close to his own release.

"I'm going to give you what you want, beautiful, but don't come until you get permission," Blake said, beginning to pump in and out, slowly at first, but with enough force that Erin's ass rippled every time he thrust home. "If you come before, I'm going to use those clothespins on your pussy."

"Yes, God, yes." She gasped and her breath came faster as his rhythm increased.

The desire in her voice was nearly enough to make Blake laugh, no matter how close he was to the edge. He should have known Erin wouldn't consider clamps on her pussy lips a punishment. She was into a little bit of pain. He could understand the kink completely. He enjoyed pain himself. He couldn't wait to feel her teeth on him again, raking across his lips, digging into his bicep as she writhed beneath him.

"Don't come, Erin." Blake punctuated his words with a sharp smack on her white ass and then another and another. He began to spank her in earnest, reddening her beautiful ass until her flesh was swollen and every thrust of his cock into her pussy made her moan.

"Please, Blake," she begged, her breath coming so fast he feared she might hyperventilate. "Please, I can't hold back."

"You can. You will," he said, abandoning the last of his control, holding nothing back as he drove into her slick sheath. "Wait for me, baby. Wait."

Faster and faster he moved, ramming inside

Erin even as he reddened her ass until his hand itched and stung. She cried out and shoved back into his strokes, her fingernails digging into the carpet, desperate little grunts sounding at the back of her throat as she got closer and closer, until finally he knew she couldn't hold back a second longer.

"Come, baby, come on my cock." He groaned as Erin screamed his name and her pussy squeezed his dick.

Seconds later, he lost himself inside her, thick jets pulsing from his aching sac with a bliss that was almost painful. This time, he didn't pull out, but spent himself deep inside her welcoming heat, the sensation of marking her insides with his cum making the orgasm hotter than any he could remember. Blake's entire body shook with the force of his release, turning his bones to jelly by the time the waves of pleasure finally began to abate.

"Fuck, baby," he panted as he fell forward, palms landing on either side of Erin's. He buried his face in the sweat-dampened hair at her neck and inhaled the intoxicating scent of aroused woman. "I love fucking you."

"I love getting fucked," she said, her voice breathy with laughter. "That was perfect. Just what I needed."

"I'm sorry I couldn't make you come twice." Blake wrapped one arm around her waist and pulled her closer, relishing the feel of his cock softening inside her. "I knew I wouldn't last through more than one, you felt too amazing."

"But what a one it was." She sighed as she twined the fingers of her left hand with his. "I'm not greedy, one can be plenty. Though, next time, let's skip the next to the fire thing. It's romantic, but I'm a little dizzy from the heat."

"I thought it was my superior fucking skills."

She laughed. "That probably has something to do with it, too." She shifted beneath him, dropping her forehead to the carpet. "I actually don't mind the dizziness, but the dripping sweat I could do without."

"I don't know, I like a little sweat." He ran his tongue along her shoulder, catching the lightly salty taste of her with his tongue.

"Me too, until it dries and starts to feel sticky and gross."

"Hint taken." Blake pulled out of Erin and sat back on his heels, watching her as she rolled over to face him. "What would you say to a shower?"

"I'd love one." She met his eyes with an almost shy look that absolutely slayed him. "I'm assuming this shower will be coed?"

"Of course. I wouldn't want you to have to clean your own back...or my pussy." He stood and reached down to help Erin to her feet, marveling that even something as simple as taking her hand sent a shock of electricity through his body. "Besides, someone has to show you how to work the shower nozzle."

"Oh, I know how," she said with a soft laugh. "In fact, I think I could show you a few things, mister." She reached her hand between his legs, cupping his sac and rolling his balls in her fingers. "I could do some nice things to these in massage mode."

"I bet you could." He groaned and bent down to capture her lips.

She met his tongue with her own, sighing as they explored each other with a sweetness that surprised him. No matter how intense the fucking had been, the tender mood they'd established before hadn't been destroyed. In fact, if anything, he loved her more than he had a few minutes ago.

"I love you," he mumbled against her lips. "And I'm not going to stop saying it. If it scares you, you'll have to get over it."

"I'll try." She wrapped her arms around his torso and hugged him, pressing her breasts and the clothespins still attached to them against his chest.

"Are you ready for those to come off?" he asked, cupping the underside of her breast in one hand. "They must be stinging by now."

"I like stinging, but, yeah. They need to

come off if you're going to soap my nipples." She pulled away from him wincing as he removed the pins. "And once you've done my nipples, you should get my breasts all slick and soapy and fuck them in the shower. I heard something about a man wanting to fuck some tits a while back. That *was* you, right?"

Blake lunged for her and Erin squealed and made a run for the stairs, her squeals turning to laughter as he chased her straight into the shower.

They stepped inside and turned on the water without waiting for it to get hot, clinging to each other for the first few chilly minutes. Then, when the cool stream had warmed, Erin reached for the soap and turned back to him with a smile. A smile that promised everything naughty and nice, and everything Blake hadn't dared to hope for.

His deepest, most secret wish was coming true. Erin was going to be his, and this time he was never going to let her go.

No matter what he had to do to keep her.

CHAPTER FIFTEEN

Erin

Erin indulged in a full body stretch, luxuriating in the softness of Blake's featherbed. Her body ached in all sorts of forgotten places, but it was the soreness along her jaw muscles that shocked her the most.

When was the last time she'd smiled so much it made her face hurt? Had that *ever* happened?

But then why shouldn't she be smiling?

A few feet away, a gorgeous man who had made her come twice in the shower and two more times once they'd stumbled into his bedroom was digging through his suitcase and making noises about cooking tortellini for dinner. Every once in a while, he turned around to smile at her as he plucked jeans and a tight brown sweater from the neatly folded clothes in his bag and pulled them on, the look in his eyes leaving no doubt that he loved her.

He loved her.

Blake still *loved* her and wanted them to have a future together.

The thought was exhilarating…and completely terrifying. She felt the same way about him and he seemed to be everything she'd ever wanted in a partner, but there was still that shred of doubt.

What would he do when he found out the mess she'd gotten herself into with her ex? No matter how much he loved her, she knew it would be hard for Blake to respect her once he realized she'd willingly turned her entire life over to a man she'd barely known for six months before they were married. He would think she was a fool. Hell, *she* thought she was a fool, so she couldn't really blame him.

And even if he could look past her poor decisions, what would Blake do when he found out she wasn't flying solo anymore? That she came with extra baggage in the form of a nearly one-year-old little girl?

Would he still want her when he found out the truth?

And even if he did, would he be able to really *love* another man's child? Erin couldn't imagine building a life with a man who couldn't love her little girl as much as she did. She wanted Abby to grow up feeling treasured by everyone around her. And if that meant Erin was destined to be alone for the rest of her life, so be it. When she finally got her daughter back, she was going to make whatever sacrifices were necessary to ensure

Abby had the happy, healthy childhood she and Blake hadn't.

Even if that meant giving up her second chance with the man of her dreams.

"I'm going down to start supper," Blake said, turning back to her with a pile of clothes in his large hands.

Erin forced a smile, not wanting him to see the direction her thoughts had been taking. "What's this?"

"I brought you jeans, a sweater, and a long-sleeved tee shirt for underneath," he said. "In case the sweater's itchy. Size two on the jeans and small on everything else. Is that about right?"

"That's perfect." She took the clothes from his hands, marveling at the softness of the pale blue sweater. It was obviously expensive, which made her sad. She'd been with Scott for years and he'd never spent money on clothes for her. Pricey lingerie, yes, but that had been more for his pleasure than her own.

"Just about perfect." Blake reached out and

tucked a piece of hair behind her ear with a smile. "A little skinny, but I can help you take care of that. I'm a decent cook."

"You're an amazing cook, but you can't fatten me up until I get some modeling work," she said with a sigh. "I've got bills to pay, and people prefer their models bony."

"What people?" he scoffed. "Real men like women who look healthy, curvy, and happy." He smiled as he moved toward the stairs. "Besides, I've got enough money to take care of your bills, don't worry about it."

"Blake," Erin said, waiting until he stopped and turned back to her before continuing. "I don't want you to pay my bills. I care about you and I love submitting to you, but I've learned there are aspects of my life that I need to be in control of myself."

He nodded. "All right. But let me know if you change your mind. I'd love to help you if you decide to let me," he said, the matter clearly dismissed. "Now hurry up and get dressed. I'm going to put you to work chopping vegetables. Can't have you thinking you'll be waited on every meal."

"Yes, sir." Erin smiled and made a show of leaping out of the bed and scrambling into her jeans, making Blake laugh before he headed down the stairs.

As soon as he was gone, however, she felt her spirits deflate and sank back down onto the bed.

The fact that he'd so easily understood what had been a huge point of contention early in her marriage to Scott only made her more anxious. Blake really was the man she'd been dreaming about, the type of Dom who understood that being in control of a submissive didn't mean taking charge of every aspect of her life. She knew he'd never try to make her sign the kind of contract Scott had, the one that gave the Dominant partner control over his submissive's finances as well as everything else.

Men like Blake didn't need that kind of stranglehold on another person to feel powerful.

"Right, and how stupid is he going to think you are for signing something like that in the first place?" Erin dropped her face into her hands.

When had this weekend become so complicated? She certainly had a gift for getting herself into impossible situations.

This isn't impossible, just impractical and crazy and doomed from the start.

Damned inner voice. No sense in sitting around listening to it prophesy certain disaster.

Erin stood and shrugged on the long-sleeved tee and sweater—which was one hundred percent angora from Neiman Marcus, so her expensive vibes had been right on the money—and headed into the bathroom to try to do something with her hair. She worked a little of Blake's gel through the still damp curls and then dug through her purse for lipstick and mascara. She wanted to look pretty for Blake, to relax and enjoy the rest of their time at the cabin together, but she knew she had to come clean sooner or later.

There was no point in stressing out about what he would think of her stupider decisions, or foretelling the end of their relationship before they'd even gotten started on their second chance. She needed to talk to him, tell him everything, and let him make his own decisions about what he could or couldn't deal with in a woman he was dating.

Dating.

It was a strange word to think of in conjunction with her and Blake. They weren't dating kind of people. Their relationship was already too intense for such a casual term. After only a day, she couldn't breathe as easily when he wasn't in the room. Blake could quickly become a person she depended on, someone she needed as much as she needed anything in the world.

Dangerous, scary thoughts there, Erin.

"Well, life can be scary. And not everything worth having is easy," she said to her reflection as she coated her lashes with dark brown mascara.

That's what you said about Scott. Look how that turned out.

"Oh, shut up. Just shut up." Erin threw her mascara back into her purse.

Great, now she was yelling at the voices in her head. She had to nip this in the bud.

Before she could talk herself out of it, Erin turned toward the stairs. She would go down to the kitchen and tell Blake everything. Right now. Before they ate tortellini, before she fell any more head over heels for him than she was already. Even if telling the truth meant she would lose him, at least she would know how this was going to end.

She couldn't handle any more suspense. Suspense was one of her least favorite things, unless it was of the sexual variety.

She was nearly to the bottom of the stairs when she heard Blake talking and froze. For a moment, she thought someone else must have arrived at the cabin, but after a few seconds it became clear he was on the phone. She hadn't seen a landline in any of the rooms, so it must be his cell. Which made her wonder if her own cell was getting reception.

Some smarty-pants she was. And here she'd thought that stellar grade on her GED and As in the classes she'd taken at the community college had meant something. But if she'd really been focused on getting out of here and away from her captor, checking her cell reception should have been the first thing she did the moment she was alone.

Of course, that was the problem. She hadn't wanted to get away, not really. Not even when she'd run from Blake on the side of the road. Even as she'd run for the headlights coming around the corner, she'd wanted him to catch her.

"Yeah, I need a complete background check. I want to see what she's been up to," Blake said to the person at the other end of the line.

Background check? On her? Dear God,

what did he think she'd been doing for the past eight years that required a *background* check? *He* was the one who had turned into a kidnapper.

"See if there's any criminal record, and if so, what she was charged with."

Oh. My. God.

Erin sagged against the stair railing.

Blake thought she was a criminal, and was making sure she wasn't dangerous before he took things any further in their relationship. The lack of trust implied by the background check he'd just ordered was...staggering. She'd trusted him not to hurt her and submitted to him without question, even after he'd told her he intended to mark her body without her permission. And yet *he* was the one who felt the need to do a background check.

It didn't just hurt her feelings; it made her angry.

Really angry. With Blake, but more importantly, with herself.

She should have known better. After years in a horrible Dom-sub relationship, she'd been ready to jump right back into another one in less than a day. It didn't matter that Blake wasn't a stranger and the first boy she'd ever loved, he was still a person she'd had no contact with for the past eight years. She should have insisted on moving forward slowly if they were going to move forward at all. Going to bed with your kidnapper hours after getting into his car and professing your love for him twenty-four hours later was insane. She obviously needed some kind of intensive therapy.

Which she was going to make sure she signed up for, as soon as she got the hell away from Blake Roberts.

CHAPTER SIXTEEN

Blake

Blake went ahead and chopped the tomatoes, garlic, and fresh basil himself. Erin was taking forever upstairs, but he didn't want to rush her. She'd said something about wanting to fix her hair and makeup before dinner and he knew how long those girlish things could take. And even though he thought she was just as beautiful without makeup and with her hair in

185

crazy curls, knowing she wanted to dress up just for him made him smile.

A lot.

Smiling and humming beneath his breath, he put the tortellini on to boil and fetched the pine nuts, fresh mozzarella, and baby green beans from the fridge.

Everything was working out amazingly well. This weekend was turning out to be one of the best of his entire life. He felt so comfortable with Erin. Spending time with her was like going home, to a real home. To that place of warmth and love and happiness neither one of them had ever known.

And the sex was…indescribable. He hadn't realized he could come so hard, so often. She made him wild with a single look, the slightest touch. He could fuck her every day for the rest of his life and never get tired of feeling her body pressed against him. She was everything he'd ever dreamed of and everything he'd ever need. He knew he was crazy, but he was already thinking forever and wondering how long he'd have to wait before he asked her to move in with him.

Blake's phone buzzed in his pocket. It was Rafe calling him back. It hadn't been more than fifteen minutes since they hung up the first time, but his partner had some excellent sources. Rafe's ability to get the dirt on just about anyone sometimes made Blake a little suspicious.

Rafe used to be a police officer before he quit to do the tattoo artist thing full-time, but sometimes it seemed too easy for him to find out the personal details of other people's lives. Even police officers had to work to get access to things like juvenile arrests and medical records.

Especially medical records.

But when Rafe had discovered a girl Blake was casually dating was HIV-positive and hiding it from her lovers in order to convince them to indulge her passion for blood play, Blake hadn't asked questions. He hadn't cared how Rafe had gotten the information; he'd just been glad to learn the truth before he'd put himself at risk.

The same was true now. Before he got in any deeper with Erin, he had to know what she was hiding and whether he could help her out of whatever trouble she was in. If not, he didn't know if he could handle getting any closer to the woman upstairs. If she'd gotten herself into a bad situation beyond his control to remedy, it would drive him insane. He couldn't deal with seeing her suffer and not being able to keep her safe.

"What did you find out?" Blake asked, keeping his voice low in case Erin made an appearance. Surely she was nearly ready by now and would be headed down the stairs any second.

"Nothing much. It's like the woman dropped out of her life a few years ago," Rafe said. "I found a couple of pictures from her wedding to this Scott Sack of Potatoes guy, but—"

"What?"

"Sakapatatis." Rafe snorted. "No wonder Erin didn't change her name. That has to be one of the least sexy last names I've ever heard. It would have been lingerie model suicide."

Blake sighed and rolled his eyes. "So that's it? Her ex has a lame last name? That's all you found out?"

"No, that's not all I found out. This is me you're talking to." Rafe sniffed, clearly offended. "She has a clean criminal record. Never even had an unpaid parking ticket, which probably wasn't too hard considering she didn't have a driver's license until about two months ago."

Blake frowned. "No driver's license?"

"Not in California, and the Nevada license expired years ago."

"That's strange," he muttered. Erin had always loved to drive his car and had been at the DMV the morning of her sixteenth birthday ready to test for her license.

"And it gets stranger, my friend," Rafe said.

"According to her and Sack of Potatoes' tax records, she reported no income from the time she quit modeling until she started working at the bar. Absolutely nothing."

Blake sighed. "Maybe he didn't want her to work. From what I've heard, he sounds like the type."

"Maybe. But he didn't want her to spend, either." Rafe paused and Blake heard the sound of computer keys clicking in the background. "Her name wasn't on any of his four bank accounts and she didn't have an account of her own. She didn't even have a credit card. There's no credit history on the chick for the past few years."

Blake grunted, putting the pieces together before Rafe spoke again.

"Which probably means she's flat-ass broke, brother. Unless she's been stashing cash under her mattress or something."

"What about the money she earned modeling?" Blake asked, turning down the heat on the tortellini. "What happened to that? She must have had an account before she was married."

"She did," Rafe said, irritation creeping into his tone. "But she closed it out before she hooked up with her husband. She's broke, man. Like, two bad calls away from being on the street broke."

"So what?" Blake snapped.

"So nothing! Don't shoot the messenger, brother. If you want to sign on to be her sugar daddy, that's your business." He paused for a moment, but Blake could tell there was something still left unsaid.

"What aren't you telling me?" Blake asked, trying to keep the frustration out of his voice as he poured the tortellini into the colander to drain. "I don't have a lot of time right now, Rafe."

His friend sighed. "Fine. She's got a kid, okay. A baby."

"What?" Blake dropped the pot into the sink with a clatter.

If Erin had a baby, who was taking care of

him or her while she was up here with him? The thought of an infant, left with some babysitter, wondering where his or her mother was made his stomach bottom out.

"She's eleven months old," Rafe said. "Abigail Diana Sakapatatis. From what I can find, it seems like she's living with Erin's husband."

"But he was abusive to Erin, I'm almost certain of it."

Rafe made a considering sound. "Yeah, well, maybe she had to get out, you know, but couldn't take the kid with her. If she has no money, she wouldn't be equipped to—"

"No way." Blake's free hand balled into a fist. "She would never leave her child with someone like that. She just wouldn't."

"Listen, don't freak out on me. I'm just telling you what I learned." Rafe sighed, and Blake could tell he wasn't going to like the next words out of his partner's mouth. "And I'll tell you something else, I think you're crazy. You don't know this woman anymore.

She is not the same sweet little girl you fell in love with."

"You don't know anything about her."

"No, but I do know a thing or two about you," Rafe countered. "And I know that, beneath that big bad act, you're a softie, man. You're a prime target for a woman like her."

"Choose your next words very carefully," Blake warned.

"I'm not saying anything bad about your precious Erin," the other man said, his eye roll audible in his tone. "I'm just saying she's a woman who is clearly in trouble. Financial trouble and probably more, if this soon-to-be ex is as bad as you think."

"Again, so what?"

Rafe drew in a calming breath, and when he spoke again, his voice was softer. "So help her if you want to help her, but don't let yourself think you two are headed for couples-ville. She's clearly in no place to start a relationship."

"I'm going to hang up now." Blake could

barely force the words out through his clenched jaw. Rafe didn't know what he was talking about. He'd never dated the same woman for more than a month at a time, what did he know about relationships?

"Fine," Rafe said, tightly. "But when she uses you and leaves your ass a second time, don't say I didn't warn—"

Blake snapped the phone closed and threw it across the room to land on the couch. He shouldn't have brought the damned thing. He hadn't wanted any distractions when he came to the mountains. That's why he hadn't had a landline installed in the first place.

The last thing he'd needed was a dose of reality via Rafe, the biggest cynic in his personal acquaintance. Blake was the one whose mother had dumped him on his dad's porch before he could even walk and never come back. Then his dad, the only adult who had ever made Blake feel safe and cared for, had died when he was ten and he'd been shuffled from shitty foster home to shittier foster home until he was eighteen.

Still, Rafe was the one who acted like life had betrayed him. Blake had never met the other man's family, but they must be some pieces of work to make Rafe distrust people even more than he did.

"Erin? Are you about ready?" Blake shouted to be heard upstairs as he fished the wok out from the cupboard and dumped the tortellini and vegetables inside. "We're about two minutes from pasta arrival."

Silence. Not so much as the sound of footsteps crossing the floor or water running in the bathroom.

"Erin?" he called again.

Still nothing, the kind of nothing that made the hairs stand up on his arms and his throat grow tight. Blake set the wok on the stove but didn't turn on the burner. Instead, he headed for the stairs, wiping his damp hands on his jeans as he went.

There had to be a logical explanation. Maybe she had found the iPod in his suitcase and was checking out his playlists. Erin had always loved to play her music loud and he doubted becoming a mom had changed that.

A mom. Erin was a mom.

A mom who had left her little girl with a potentially dangerous man. The knowledge all but killed the spark of pleasure the idea of meeting Erin's daughter had inspired.

What could have driven her to make that kind of decision? Was she so traumatized by her marriage that she wanted out any way she could, even if that meant leaving her daughter behind? Maybe she'd wanted to take her baby with her, but hadn't had the money, as Rafe had suggested.

Or maybe she just hadn't taken to being a parent the way he'd always thought she would.

They'd never really talked about kids in-depth, but even as a teenager Erin had seemed like the kind of woman who would grow up to be a great mother. The way she'd taken care of the younger foster kids in Phil's house had always impressed him. She hadn't just made sure they had something to eat or helped them with homework, she'd done her best to make them smile, to lessen the negative impact of living with Phil in her own small way.

Could she have changed so much in eight years?

Blake had to find out. She'd probably be pissed that he'd snooped around behind her back, but he intended to talk this through. Tonight.

He turned the corner, and his stomach dropped

"Erin?" He said her name one last time, even though the open window next to Erin's bed assured him she wouldn't be answering his call.

She was gone.

CHAPTER SEVENTEEN

Erin

Erin burst out of the woods just as the sun was setting, painting the woods in soft rose light with dark blue shadows gathering beneath the trees.

Despite the cold mountain air, sweat dripped down the valley of her spine. Her face was scratched from fighting her way through the low-hanging limbs and her jeans were soaked through to the knee from wading through the snowdrifts. But at least she'd made it to the edge of the little town where she'd glimpsed lights shining the night before.

She hadn't dared take the road. It would have taken too much time and Blake would have found her for sure. Even now, he might still find a way to stop her. He had to have realized she was gone and put two and two together to guess where she'd go now that she had her freedom. The town at the bottom of the ravine was the only sign of civilization, and the only place where she might find someone to help her.

"Or a bus station, if I'm lucky." Erin took a deep breath and exhaled a puff of white. The temperature was falling fast.

Even warm from her run and wearing a heavy sweater, she was starting to feel the cold. Luckily the boots Blake had brought for her seemed to be waterproof, but her jeans were not. The damp fabric felt like it was freezing to the skin beneath. She had to find a place to get inside and get warmed up before she risked frostbite—hopefully that bus station she was dreaming about. A bus ticket and a snug little waiting room that served hot chocolate would be heaven right now.

Or maybe something a little stronger than hot chocolate. An Irish coffee sounded good. Anything to help numb the pain and anxiety flooding through her system. She'd only spent a *day* with Blake, but leaving him was as horrible as it had been the first time. Far worse than leaving the man she'd been married to for years.

But she couldn't think about that now. She had to focus on getting the hell out of Dodge.

Erin set a swift pace down the street toward a line of wooden buildings resembling the main drag of an Old West town. She was still too far away to know for certain, but the businesses appeared to be mostly souvenir shops and outdoor supply stores. There were only a few cars parked alongside the street, but, hopefully, that meant there were a few townspeople who hadn't headed home for dinner yet. Surely one of them would be willing to give her a ride to the bus station. Or at least let her use their phone to call someone to help her if there wasn't a station in town.

Her cell had died sometime between leaving L.A. and arriving in the mountains. She must have forgotten to charge it before she went to work Friday night. Stupid and careless, but she hadn't anticipated being gone from home more than a few hours. She certainly hadn't imagined being kidnapped and ending up in a sleepy mountain town desperate to make contact with one of her few friends in Los Angeles.

They hadn't known each other long, but she was guessing Cassandra from the bar wouldn't mind driving a few hours to pick her up, as long as Erin paid for her gas and spilled all the sordid details of how she'd ended up stranded in the middle of nowhere. Cassie lived for gossip whether it be the Hollywood variety sold at grocery store checkouts or the intimate details of her friends' and coworkers' lives. She'd break every speed limit between L.A. and wherever the hell Erin was calling from as soon as she heard the words "kidnapped" and "ex-lover" in the same sentence.

The idea of the ride home with Cassie, however, made Erin pray there was a bus station close by. She didn't want to talk about what had happened with her and Blake. Not now, maybe not ever.

She broke into a jog, swiftly closing the distance to the only business still open this late in the winter months. Skiing was a big tourist draw in these parts, but a little town at the bottom of a ravine too steep for the skiing and snowboarding enthusiasts to maneuver probably didn't see much action once the sun went down. The tourists all flocked back to Arrowhead or Big Bear to eat and drink away the chill from a day spent on the slopes.

But even a tiny town like this one had the requisite mom-and-pop diner, serving eggs and pancakes in the morning and other down-home favorites the rest of the day. The blackboard nailed to the wall outside proclaimed today's special to be chicken fried steak with potatoes and gravy and green beans.

Erin's stomach rumbled, despite the fact that chicken fried steak would no doubt be a pathetic meal compared to the pasta Blake had been preparing for them up in his cabin. He'd told her he'd brought a bottle of Merlot to go with the food and cheesecake for dessert, and sounded so excited to share both with her.

To share the evening with her, period.

But how could he have really felt that way if he'd been so desperate to invade her privacy the second her back was turned? And not just invade her privacy by himself, but ask some friend of his to do it, to delve into her past and find out if she was a *criminal*, for God's sake.

It made her wonder what he'd really

thought of her all those years ago. If he'd known her as well as she'd thought, surely he would have realized she would never do anything illegal.

Scandalous and wild, yes. Reckless and stupid, probably. But not illegal. That wasn't her. Never had been, never would be.

The sound of a car pulling down the road behind her made Erin press closer to the wall of the diner, hoping the awning shading the entrance would conceal her. With her blond hair and light blue sweater, it wouldn't be that difficult to spot her from the road. And if Blake saw her, she was as good as caught. There was no one on the street to hear her scream for help, even if she managed to call out before he hustled her into the Expedition.

A quick peek over her shoulder revealed a beat-up Jeep trundling down the road, not Blake's Expedition. She was safe for now, but the clock was ticking.

Blake was coming for her; she could feel it in her gut. He wouldn't let her go without a fight, she knew that much. He'd feel betrayed that she'd run, as betrayed as she'd felt when she'd discovered how little he trusted the woman he professed to love.

But she should have known better than to fall for that so fast. It didn't matter how much history they had. He was a stranger and she'd proven her heart should never be allowed out of the cage she'd put it in the past two years.

A bell rang above the door as Erin pushed inside the diner. The smells of frying meat and homemade bread engulfed her, making her stomach rumble again. It had been a long time since brunch and she and Blake had made sure she'd worked up a hearty appetite.

Erin's muscles ached from their marathon lovemaking as much as her run down the mountainside. But those aches would fade in a few days' time. No telling how long the aching in her chest would last. Her stupid heart had already grown ridiculously attached to Blake again.

So attached it raced with excitement, not

fear, when a large hand suddenly closed around her wrist.

"I figured you'd come here. Only place in town open after five during the winter." Blake's eyes were dark and expressionless, but Erin could feel the anger in the iron grip of his fingers.

"Let go of me. I'm going home," Erin said, keeping her voice low so as not to attract any more attention from the few diners scattered throughout the small restaurant. People were already staring, no need to make a scene.

Yet.

But if Blake didn't take no for an answer...

"You're going back to the cabin with me," Blake rumbled in his deep, dangerous voice. "I'm going to do what we came here to do. Right now. Afterward, I'll drive you home myself. Tonight if you want."

"What I want is for you to let me go." Erin tried to jerk away, but he held her tight. "I'm not going back to the cabin, and I'm not letting you touch me again. With a tattoo

207

needle or anything else."

"You'll do what I ask you to do for the next few hours," he assured her, his tone making her shiver.

"I'm not playing games anymore, Blake," Erin said, hoping he read the truth in her eyes. "I will not obey you, I will not submit to you, and I'm not going anywhere with you willingly. You'll have to use force."

"I don't have a problem with that." His eyes glittered with anger and something else, something that looked a lot like hurt.

"Well, I do. Try to drag me out of here and I will scream for help," she whispered. "I'll tell these people to call the police and you'll end up spending the night in jail."

Blake made a sound halfway between a grunt and a growl. "That was your plan all along, wasn't it? Act like you cared about me, get me to lower my guard, and then make a run for it?"

"Yep. Sure was." Erin hoped the words hurt him as much as he'd hurt her.

That *had* been her plan at first. No need to let him know how her plan had changed, how she'd started to dream about the future they were going to have together.

"Like I said before," Blake said. "You're a great actress. You had me completely fooled."

Erin flinched despite herself. Angry Blake she could deal with, but hurt Blake made her feel like she was being gutted by the pain in his words. It was almost enough to make her tell him the truth—that she'd been as fooled as he was until she'd heard him on the phone checking into her criminal background.

Criminal background.

The thought made her grit her teeth. Anger banished the last of her guilt. This man didn't know her and didn't trust her. Talking would be futile.

"That must have been hard for you, pretending to be attracted to me, to be falling in love with me again," Blake said, his grip on her wrist growing so tight Erin flinched again, this time in pain.

"You're hurting me."

"Good." His eyes grew colder, but his fingers gentled on her arm.

Erin took the opportunity to jerk her hand free and back a few steps away.

"You should go." She crossed her arms and stuck her chin in the air, willing herself not to show how upset she was. "People are starting to stare."

Blake took a menacing step forward. "Let them stare. I'm not going anywhere without you, even if I have to throw you over my shoulder and carry you back to the car."

"So I guess you want to go to jail," Erin said, a part of her wanting to slap the stubborn expression off of his face.

What was he thinking? This was insane. He couldn't abduct her *again* in front of half a dozen people and expect to get away with it. He really would be arrested if he tried that.

"Is that why you kidnapped me in the first place?" she asked. "You have dreams of a life behind bars?"

"I'll give you one last chance, Erin." Blake stilled, watching her like a predator stalking prey he had no doubt he would catch. Eventually. "Walk with me to the car, or I'm going to carry you out."

"You're crazy if you think—" Erin's words ended in a gasp as Blake did exactly as he'd threatened, scooping her over his shoulder in one smooth movement and turning toward the door.

"No! Put me down!" She yelled, pounding on his back with her fists.

How dare he? She was not a child or a dog who'd run off into the woods!

She was an adult who—no matter what her sexual preferences were—deserved to be treated with respect and to have people listen when she said "no." Her husband might never have gotten that message, but Blake sure as hell would. She'd send the bastard to jail and see how *he* enjoyed having his free will stolen away.

"Help!" she screamed as Blake swung out

onto the street. "Someone, call the—"

Blake's hand covered her mouth, cutting off her words. Erin could only pray someone in the diner knew where he lived and would call for help. In the meantime, she would continue to fight for her freedom.

She wasn't going to passively submit to Blake—or anyone else—ever again.

Read the conclusion to Blake and Erin's story in CLAIMING HER HEART.

Keep reading for a sneak peek

Acknowledgements

I really do have so many people to thank, so please forgive my gushing in advance.

Big thanks to my husband, my biggest fan and most tireless supporter. You believed I could do this when not many people did. Love you hard man, forever and ever. Let's never go our separate ways.

Thank you to my critique partners (the most patient women in the world) for reading numerous drafts and never getting tired of Erin and Blake (or at least not letting me know they were tired of them).

Thank you to my editor, proofers, and sweet and lovely cover designer—this wouldn't have been possible without you!

Big huge thanks to all the readers out there. You are rock stars. The way you go above and beyond to support the authors you enjoy is truly amazing and so appreciated. Much, much love and endless thanks for embracing a newbie and making me one of your own.

Mad thanks to Kara H. for keeping me organized and on task. Without your help, professionalism, and all around awesome the launch for the Under His Command series wouldn't have gone one fifth as smoothly. You are the best!

Thanks to all the early reviewers who took a chance on Controlling Her Pleasure. I appreciate your time and effort to post ratings and reviews so much.

Finally a few special shout outs:

To my street team: You are the sweetest, naughtiest, book-loving-est people ever and I feel so lucky to have you in my life.

To Lauren Blakely who is a genius and a talent and just as importantly, a woman with a kind and generous heart. Thanks for being a friend and inspiration.

To Monica Murphy. Who would have thought we'd be here when we met in 2005? Can't wait to hang out with you again soon and soak up more of that signature MM sweetness and sass.

To Sawyer Bennett, a talented and generous new friend who constantly inspires me to be a better, more chill person. You make it look easy, doll.

To Violet Duke for the amazing cover design, friendship, and support—even though I write naughty books and yours are so sweet and wonderful they make me laugh and cry in equal measure. You are a blessing to all who know you and that's the truth.

To Robin, friend and editorial guru, you make me laugh and keep my commas under control. Without you I would wander in the darkness of WTF punctuation-ville.

To my mother, who told to me to write whatever I wanted to write and pay no attention to the naysayers. What a lucky chick I am to have a mama like you.

To my father, who didn't live to meet my husband, babies, or book babies, but who raised me to believe I could do whatever I set my mind to, as long as I was willing to work hard and never give up. Thank you, Dad. You are missed more than you know.

And on a much lighter note, thank you to all the makers of chocolate in all its wondrous forms. You lift me up on days when the sun doesn't shine.

LILI VALENTE

Tell Lili your favorite part!

Lili loves feedback from her readers.

If you could take a moment to leave a review letting her know your favorite part of the story—nothing fancy required, even a sentence or two would be wonderful—she would be deeply grateful.

Reviews are so important and help other readers discover new authors and series to enjoy.

About the Author

Lili Valente started writing naughty books in her early twenties as a way to unwind after a long day in the day job trenches. She soon learned there was nothing more fun than torturing fictional characters who have dynamite chemistry in the bedroom.

After a prolonged detour through other areas of writing and publishing—including a short stint as a news reporter for a small town paper—she's back to penning red hot stories and loving every minute of it.

She lives on an island in the middle of nowhere, where she eats entirely too much fish and drinks more than her fair share of dark, island rum.

Lili has slept under the stars in Greece, eaten dinner at midnight with French men who couldn't be trusted to keep their mouths on their food, and walked alone through Munich's red light district after dark and lived to tell the tale.

These days you can find her writing in a tent beside the sea, drinking coconut water and thinking delightfully dirty thoughts.

Lili loves to hear from her readers.!

You can reach her via email at lili.valente.romance@gmail.com

Or like her page on Facebook https://www.facebook.com/AuthorLiliVal

ente?ref=hl

You can also visit her website:
www.lilivalente.com

Or sign up for her newsletter here:
http://bit.ly/1zXpwL6

Claiming Her Heart Under His Command Book 3

Warning: Dominant alpha hero Blake Roberts will own your nights and forever ruin you for lesser men

Blake has what he thought he wanted—Erin's submission, her trust, and the woman he loves back in his bed. But with her submission comes protection of her secrets. Erin is in trouble and an innocent life hangs in the balance. Blake knows he can help her break free of the past, but he doesn't know if a man like himself belongs in her future.

How can he swear to protect her from danger when he has a dark side of his own?

Please enjoy this free excerpt of **CLAIMING HER HEART,** Under His Command Book Three

Available March 16th, 2015 via Createspace, Amazon, and Barnes and Noble.

CHAPTER ONE

Blake

Erin was nearly naked again, wearing nothing but tiny black panties.

Her jeans had been soaked through or he wouldn't have taken them off. Blake needed her shirt off to get to the tattoo, but not her pants.

It certainly would be easier to concentrate if she were wearing more clothes and didn't look so damned sexy spread out, face down, on the bed in his room. He still wanted her as much as he always had—probably always would—but the time for making love or

229

fucking or whatever they'd been doing was over.

From this point on, he was all business.

Too bad this business had a lot in common with one of his favorite pleasures…

Bondage had always been a huge turn-on, even before he discovered the BDSM lifestyle. Either binding his lover or being bound himself, it didn't much matter. Both made Blake hard enough to shatter rock.

It was no surprise that his cock swelled uncomfortably within the confines of his jeans as he cuffed Erin's wrists to the mission-style headboard of the bed. He couldn't help being aroused, but he could have kept his hands to himself.

But he couldn't seem to resist tracing the column of her spine with his fingertips, past the small of her back and down both of her legs. He couldn't keep from gripping her just above the knees, digging his fingers into the soft flesh with the perfect amount of pressure, the kind he knew made Erin's pussy gush.

And then her pulled her thighs apart.

Wide.

Wider…spreading her open for him before he moved his fingers to her ankles.

A soft moan of excitement escaped Erin's lips as he knelt between her legs, making Blake's breath rush out softly in relief. Ever since he'd thrown her over his shoulder at the diner, he'd felt like a monster, a feeling that had only gotten worse as she continued to fight him all the way up to the cabin. With every passing second, he'd become increasingly convinced that he'd gone too far, crossed the line between consensual power exchange and being a goddamned bully.

But that sigh of arousal helped calm his fears.

No matter what she'd said in the diner or on the road up to the cabin, Erin hadn't been faking her physical responses to his touch.

Her emotional response, however, was clearly another story. A story that made him so full of hurt and rage he saw red every time he thought about how easily he'd been played.

"See there, Erin. Aren't you glad I caught you in time?" His voice was as rough as the rope he used to secure first one ankle and then the other to the baseboard near her feet.

He'd only brought the one pair of cuffs so rope would have to do. At this point, the idea of rope burns on Erin's delicate skin didn't bother him as much as it would have two hours ago. It was amazing how badly it hurt to realize she'd been lying to him from the moment they'd arrived at the cabin.

He'd been a fool to believe the woman he'd *kidnapped* could have real feelings for him again in less than a day. No matter how much he cared for her, no matter how right it had felt to pick up where they'd left off eight years ago, it had been pure stupidity to drop his guard. He should have stuck to his original plan from the beginning and spared himself the heartache.

And avoided abducting Erin from a public place. Again. You've really lost it, asshole, and chances are good you'll be facing criminal charges.

His inner voice was channeling Rafe this evening.

It was a pain in his ass and, unfortunately, probably right on the money. Even if the people in the diner didn't call the police to report what they'd seen, Erin now had several witnesses to corroborate her claims of being kidnapped.

A day ago, he would have said that it didn't matter, that he wouldn't have denied the charges anyway. After all the lies and deception he'd had to deal with growing up, he was more than a fan of the truth—he was a devotee. But now a part of him would be tempted to insist this weekend trip had been a consensual affair. He was *that* angry about being taken for a ride.

Or that devastated; take your pick.

He preferred angry. It hurt a hell of a lot less.

"Tell me, Erin," he whispered, his voice thick with anger. "Now."

He finished up at her ankles and moved over her prone form, bracing his hands on either side of her shoulders, hovering close enough that he could feel the heat of her body but not the silky softness of her skin. He moved his mouth just the barest bit closer, letting his lips brush softly against the back of her neck as he spoke again. "Tell me what you want."

Erin shivered, but he could tell it wasn't from the cold. She was aroused, he would bet his hands on it. If he let his fingers slide into those tiny black panties, he'd find her wet and ready, no matter how much of a fight she'd put up as he carried her up the stairs and wrestled her onto her stomach on the bed.

"Fuck you," she whispered, anger clear in her tone.

So she was pissed as well as turned on. Good. That made two of them.

"I don't think so. No more distractions. We're going to finish this," he said, reaching over to where the tattoo machine sat beside the bed.

Blake flipped the switch on the motor then pulled on his latex gloves. He'd already prepped the gun with black ink and Erin's shoulder with an alcohol swab, so they were ready to go. All he had to do was put the needle to her skin.

He'd planned how he would modify the tat if Erin refused to give him her input, so there was no reason to stall. In half an hour, he could be finished and they could both be getting ready to head back to L.A. He should get on with it.

But for some reason, he couldn't force his hand to move any closer.

"Tell me what you want, Erin. This is your last chance," he said, hoping she heard the resolve in his voice. If she didn't talk now, she would lose the opportunity.

But she didn't say a word, only pressed her face into the quilt beneath her, every muscle tensed, bracing for the feel of the needle piercing her skin. The position only emphasized how small she was. Her wrists were tinier than ever, and her shoulder blades and the knobs of her spine were clearly visible through her skin, once more inspiring the desire to get to work fattening her up.

Fuck.

He should forget this insanity and go down and reheat the pasta, bring it upstairs, and they could eat it together in bed. They could feed each other tortellini and sips of red wine, then have each other for dessert. After all, who needed cheesecake when you could have your tongue buried in something as sweet as Erin's pussy?

The imagined scene made his cock twitch even as his throat grew uncomfortably tight. Nothing like that was ever going to happen again.

It had all been a lie, every touch, every word.

Blake's anger sharpened to a knifepoint. Erin had let him think they had a future together and made him happier than he'd been in years, only to tear him down hours later. She'd *cried* in his arms, for God's sake, wept because she was so overwhelmed by what she was feeling.

Except now he knew she hadn't been feeling anything at all. It had been an act to trick the asshole still stupid enough to be in love with a woman who couldn't give less of a shit about him.

A second later, Blake dropped the tattoo gun to her pale flesh, tracing the edge of the wing he intended to expand. He'd add enough feathers to cover the angel's body, then go to work on the face, covering the ethereal features with wild strands of black hair. By the time he was finished, no one would recognize his tat and Erin's as similar, let alone matching in every detail.

And when the resemblance was gone, he'd finally be free of this obsession that had haunted him his entire adult life.

"Stop," she sobbed.

"Sorry, I can't." He clenched his jaw,

refusing to acknowledge the guilt that whispered through his rage. Screw guilt. It wasn't going to get this job done.

"Stop it. Stop!" The words started as a whisper but ended in a scream. Erin's shout echoed off the walls of the bedroom, followed closely by the horrific sound of a woman crying.

No, she wasn't simply crying. She was wailing like her heart was breaking, weeping so hard her shoulders shook as the sobs wracked her body, ensuring there was no way he could continue the tattoo. She was shaking too badly, but more importantly, she was obviously in serious emotional distress.

He might be angry with her, but he wasn't a monster.

You're not? So, you'll strap a woman down, but not sit on her to force her to hold still.

What a fucking gentleman.

Shame swept through Blake's body like a blast of cold air, shocking him to the core.

Jesus. What was he doing?

How could he have thought he'd really be able to go through with this against Erin's will? It was madness. What's more, it was cruel. No matter what Erin had done, no matter how she'd made him feel, he was supposed to be better than this. At least, that's what he'd always told himself.

Now…he wasn't so sure.

Right now, he was behaving more like every piece of shit foster father he'd ever had than he'd imagined possible. If he looked in the mirror right now, he knew he'd see darkness in his own eyes. Darkness he'd seen in the men who had beat him, the men who'd starved their own biological kids to pay for beer, the men who had hit their wives and terrorized their families. He'd once watched his first foster dad chain a seven-year-old girl in a doghouse for the night because she'd taken the change from the couch cushions to buy candy.

That night, as ten-year-old Blake had listened to his foster sister cry and beg for someone to come get her, he had vowed he would never hurt anyone the way he'd watched so many people be hurt. He'd sworn he would be the type of man who helped people, who made their lives better.

But now he was standing above a woman he'd forcibly bound to a bed, listening to her cry.

At that moment, something inside him snapped.

He had to stop this. Now.

Before he hurt Erin any more than he already had, and before he committed an act of violence that would haunt him forever.

CPSIA information can be obtained at www.ICGtesting.com
Printed in the USA
BVOW06s1319250515

401651BV00018B/544/P